# Rocket
### & THE
## Construction
# WORKER

# Rocket
## & THE
# Construction
# WORKER

JAMES STALIKAS

*Rocket & the Construction Worker*

Copyright © 2021 by James Stalikas. All rights reserved.

No part of this publication may be reproduced, stored in a retrieval system or transmitted in any way by any means, electronic, mechanical, photocopy, recording or otherwise without the prior permission of the author except as provided by USA copyright law.

The opinions expressed by the author are not necessarily those of URLink Print and Media.

1603 Capitol Ave., Suite 310 Cheyenne, Wyoming USA 82001
1-888-980-6523 | admin@urlinkpublishing.com

URLink Print and Media is committed to excellence in the publishing industry.

Book design copyright © 2021 by URLink Print and Media. All rights reserved.

Published in the United States of America
Library of Congress Control Number: 2021916348
ISBN 978-1-64753-916-0 (Paperback)
ISBN 978-1-64753-917-7 (Digital)

21.06.21

Special thanks goes to

"God"

For giving me the ability to write and it's with great hope you'll enjoy what you read.

To Bishop R Bailey of the

"Love Gospel Assembly" On the Grand Concourse in the Bronx for his encouragement and Wisdom and support.

To my friends Cesar Roman of Shruts Plus in the Bronx. To my Son Jimmy for his Love and understanding and support.

To all the guys from local union 79 and all the building trades that know of Rocket and to all the people that lend me their ear on the 6,5,4,2,1,trains to the police and walkers of Central Park.

And last but not least I like to Thank Rocket through her love and devotion made it known to me what Love is !!!

# CONTENTS

Introduction .................................................................. 9
Chapter 1: Family, King, Squeaky & Freedom .................. 11
Chapter 2: Running Into ................................................ 25
Chapter 3: Life At The Humane Society, & Hope .............. 32
Chapter 4: Getting To Know The Gang ............................. 42
Chapter 5: King, And Showtime! ..................................... 53
Chapter 6: The Adoption ................................................ 66
Chapter 7: Jimmy And Rocket Go Home .......................... 77
Chapter 8: Jimmy & Rocket Move ................................... 89
Chapter 9: Rocket Meets Squeaky Again ......................... 101
Chapter 10: The Capture Of The Fox ............................... 112
Chapter 11: Jimmy Falls In Love ..................................... 125
Chapter 12: Rocket & The Bronx ..................................... 136
Chapter 13: Jimmy & Rocket, Eileen & Daphne ................ 148
Chapter 14: Home .......................................................... 155
About The Author .......................................................... 157

# INTRODUCTION

Hello. My name is Rocket, and I'm a Chihuahua. I'd like to express my deepest gratitude to the Humane Society of Connecticut for the love, caring and joy they showed me while I was there. I will always be grateful to them.

This is the story of how I came to be called Rocket, and how I came to love, and be loved in return. . . .

# CHAPTER 1

# Family, King, Squeaky & Freedom

I don't know how old I was, but I know I was a little puppy, all I remember there was a lot of yelling going on in the house I lived in-the house I came to call "the House of Misery."

Billy, Nick, and their dad lived in the house. Dad was the adult, but Nick and Billy were almost as big as Dad. Later, I learned they were called "teenagers." Once, I heard Nick and Billy call their dad "Dad." So I decided to call him that, too.

Billy, I felt, didn't like me very much. He used to get crazy when I went to the bathroom on the floor. I'd be in so much fear, and wonder, *Is this all there is to life? If this is it, I don't want it.*

But I had hope. So one day, when Billy asked if I wanted to go out for a bit, I was so happy that I put my two front paws up and showed my teeth. (I do that when I'm happy.) Once, I heard Billy call it "smiling." I guess that's a good word, „cause I'm happy when I do that.

Billy put my leash on me, but before we went out, Dad came home, and he started talking to Billy-loud. The next thing I remember is Billy running out of the house, and Dad looking at me really mean. Maybe he was just angry with Billy, but how could I have known that? All I know is that, whenever he looked at me like that, I was so scared, I went to the bathroom right on the floor. I did that time, too.

"No, No, don't do that!" Dad yelled, and reached up to take off his belt. "How many times must I tell you not to do that?"

He started to chase me. I ran to Billy and Nick's room and hid under the bed. The phone rang, and he stopped chasing me and went to answer it. He talked for a little while, and then I heard him say "Goodbye." The door to his room closed, and there was silence. I guess he forgot about me.

You might say I wasn't feeling too good just then. Actually, I was terrified, because I believed they were going to kill me one of these days.

I must have fallen asleep. I woke up the next morning to the sounds of birds whistling, and a nice, cool breeze came through the window. I heard Nick and Billy starting to get up. I stayed under the bed, listening to them talk. For now, at least, they weren't yelling at each other.

For some strange reason, I felt good. Why? I guess I just believed that things would be all right. " When was another story "

I heard Nick call out to me, "Sweeney, want to go out for a bit?"

But just then, I heard Dad moving in the next room. I waited because I was still scared. But when I heard Nick call out again, "Sweeney, you want to go out for a bit?" I was so happy I put my front paws up, started running around the room, showing my teeth, feeling good, and wishing it could be like this all the time. Days filled with joy and happiness instead of misery.

Nick noticed I already had my leash on. "Oh, who forgot to take your leash off?" he said. I wanted to tell him, "Billy forgot," but of course I couldn't, so I just let him grab the leash and we headed to the front door.

Once outside, we walked to his car, and Nick let go of the leash as he opened the trunk. I got a little bored, and being a curious kind of dog, I decided to do a little exploring.

As I turned the corner, I saw a few dogs across the street, playing. One of the dogs, an older German Shepard, called out to me, "Hey, little fellow over there seems like where having fun. Uh . . ."

This big guy-a German Shepherd-was talking to me, who's only a Chihuahua!

"It... It seems like you guys are having a ball," I said.

"Yeah, we're having fun now," the German Shepherd said. "But we don't know where our next meal is coming from. We don't live in a house. We have no family that wants us. So we try to get our minds off of that by jumping around and barking."

I didn't want to make him feel bad because I had a home, and he didn't. So I asked, "What's your name?" "King," he replied.

"Hi, King! My name is Sweeney," I said, and tried to think of a way to make him feel better. It wasn't easy, but finally, an idea came to me. "Tell me something, King," I said. "If you live in a house and you *still* didn't know where your next meal is coming from, and you live in fear of being beaten with a belt or even being killed someday, and you didn't know what to do with yourself... would you still be happy? So maybe you're better off not having a home."

His eyes became even sadder. "Living out here isn't all that nice. Although sometimes it's nice... no one to boss you around." He sighed. "If I had it my way, I'd rather be with a family that treated me good. And that loved me."

Just then, I heard Nick call out, "Come on, Sweeney!"

"Well, King, it's been fun, but I gotta go," I said. "The master calls and all that."

King nodded, then headed back to his gang.

I walked back to Nick and allowed him to pick up my leash. But actually, some of my own sadness was gone now. I guess it was that talk I had with King. For once, I felt like someone knew what I was talking about.

Nick shouted, "Let's go. Don't keep me waiting no more, all right?"

At that moment, the idea of being homeless wasn't scaring me like it did before. Still, I felt sorry for King. Sure, it was good to know that his owners wouldn't abuse him. Yet he didn't have a home.

Nick kept yelling at me, saying things like, "When I call you, you come. Don't ever keep me waiting again!" While he yelled, he grabbed my leash and started pulling me toward the house. He pulled so hard, my neck hurt. As he opened the door, he said, "Don't get stupid with me!"

Billy and Dad were inside, and I heard Billy say, "Is everything all right?" "Yeah, everything's fine," Nick replied.

Well, I didn't agree. But at least he didn't say anything to Dad about me wandering away. Maybe that saved me from another session with Dad and his belt.

I was kind of hungry, so I started barking at my bowl. I was only a puppy, but I had learned that sometimes, that was the only way they would feed me. Nick gave me some leftover food from the night before. But the food was spoiled-believe me, even if humans can't tell, dogs can-so I couldn't eat it. I tried doing that once, and got sick to my stomach. And it was so long before they took me outside, I guess I really made a mess of things. In fact, I think that was the first time Dad took his belt off to hit me.

But at least the water was okay.

As l was lapping up the last of the water, the kitchen door opened, and it was Dad. He looked at me and smiled.

*Wow!* I thought. *That's the first time he ever smiled at me!*

"Sweeney," he said, "want a go for a ride tomorrow?"

What do you think? I *always* want to go for a ride! I put my paws up and barked.

But after he went back into the living room, I started thinking. And I had a bad feeling mixed in with the good. Like the way I felt about living here. Sometimes it was nice. Other times, I felt like I wanted to die. But really, I just want to be loved, and give it back. Is asking for love and happiness too much? Or do I just say, "I'm the only one that's in charge of my own happiness, and I should leave here."

But I'm scared of being out there by myself. After all, I'm just a puppy. And why should I run away? I mean, I *think* they like me. They just get mad at me when I go to the bathroom on the floor, when I bark too much, when I'm hungry, or when I want to go out. And most things I do don't seem to be good enough.

*Admit it,* I told myself. *They just don't want me. So why should I hang around?* But the thought of being homeless like King and his gang kept coming to mind.

After a long day, I went under Billy's bed again. At least I had tomorrow to look forward to, when Dad will take me for a ride.

The morning came, and I could hear Dad coming. He opened the door and yelled, "Billy, Nick, get up. Today's when we take Sweeny for a ride."

After a little while, I heard the birds whistling outside, and went over to the window. The window was pretty high off the ground, but I'm good at jumping, and had already learned to jump on the stepstool under the window. From there, if I kept jumping, I could usually see what was outside. Today, I saw King and his gang out there, crossing the street in front of my house. They seemed happy, and I wasn't. So I barked at them.

King turned around and saw me. He barked back, and then the whole gang started barking. I felt great.

Behind me, Billy yelled, "Shut up!" He yelled so loud, even King heard him and started running away. I went back under the bed. At least I had a friend in King now. And that felt good.

It's strange how people can make you feel one way, and dogs can make you feel another way. But that's no good. I think people and dogs should be happy with each other. Maybe they are. Maybe most dogs don't have masters like the boys and Dad. Maybe there *are* some nice people out there, and I just haven't met them yet.

As Billy moved around the room, he saw me and said, "Sweeney, I told you to shut up, and then Dad came in and talked. And I couldn't sleep!"

"Dad came by?" Nick said as he rubbed his eyes. "What did he say?"

"He told us to get ready for Sweeny's ride," Billy said, and gave me a funny look.

Nick looked at me, and I bet his eyes were as sad as mine were. And for that moment, I felt sorry for him. Maybe he wanted to run away sometimes, too.

Some time went by, and I kept looking out the window. Almost every time, I saw King and his pack. And I kept thinking about being happy.

Nick called to me, "Here, Sweeney, here's some food for you!" It wasn't leftovers today. It was real dog food! That definitely made me happy.

When I finished my food, Nick called out, "Sweeney, wanna go out?"

I was *so* happy! *If the day is starting out like this*, I thought, *what's next?*

Nick put my leash on, and we went out. Soon, we came up to King's pack. After a while, King let out a bark, and I turned around and barked back, to say hello. Nick pulled my leash so hard, he almost took me off my feet.

The dogs must not have liked that; they started showing their teeth and growling at Nick.

"Get out of here!" Nick yelled, and then started to walk fast, pulling me toward the house. When we got there, he opened the door and pulled me inside. As he closed the door, he said, "You're safe now, Sweeney, don't worry."

I felt like telling him, "Why should I worry? They're not after me-they're after *you* for the way you pulled at my neck!" But of course, I couldn't.

"Hey, Billy," Nick yelled. "There's a pack of dogs out there. They tried to get Sweeney."

"Yeah, okay," Billy replied. "Maybe you should have let them. You could've saved us a trip."

*Saved them a trip?* Something about the way Billy said that made me feel funny, but I didn't know why.

Before I had too much more time to think, Dad came into the room, looked at me, then smiled for the second time in my life. "Hi, Sweeney," he said.

"Time to go for a ride, okay?" Then he looked at Billy and Nick. "Be ready in an hour."

# ROCKET & THE CONSTRUCTION WORKER

I've learned that I forgive people pretty easily. Especially when Nick called me onto his lap and started to rub my head. I looked into his eyes, and he looked so sad. And again, I felt bad for thinking about running away.

Dad knocked on the door. "You guys ready? Let's get going. I'll get the car."

It was a long time before Nick said, "Come on, Sweeney, come here. Good girl, let's go."

*Hey, Nick,* I thought, *it's just a ride. We'll go, and be back before you know it.*

Nick put on my leash and I followed him outside. Billy opened the back car door; I hopped in the backseat, and Nick climbed in next to me.

I heard Dad say, "Look, boys, you have to get over it. If you're not going to take care of your dog, neither am I." I saw Dad's face in the mirror. He looked mad.

As the car started moving down the street, I heard barking. Billy looked back. "Wow, look at that," he said.

I turned around. It was King and the others. King looked frightened, but I couldn't figure out why. To reassure him, I barked, *See you when I get back!*

But of course, they couldn't hear me.

Dad said, "Look at that. They're crazy, running after the car like that."

"Dad," Nick said, "they're not running after the car. They're running after Sweeney!" "Why? They know her?"

Nick sighed, "They hang out right across the street from us." "What?" Dad said. "Where we live? That little Chihuahua knows them big dogs?"

Nick nodded.

Dad's face turned mean again. "Well, they better not bother me, or else that's it for them. I'll catch them and take them to the ASPCA myself. Then they're gone!"

*ASPCA! Oh, no!* I thought. Dad had often mentioned the ASPCA to me, and from what he had said, it was an awful place. Usually, he threatened to take me there while he was taking off his belt.

The car moved some more, turning from right to left, and then Dad said, "Okay, guys, where do you want to do this? How about over there by the park?"

"Dad, let's not do this . . . please?" Nick said. "Stop it! I mean it. These dogs drive me crazy."

"Stop over there," I heard Billy say. "Pull over there."

Suddenly I wasn't feeling too good again. Something about their tone of voice scared me.

The car stopped, and we all got out.

"Dad, pretend you're looking at the engine," Nick said. "I'll take care of it." Nick pulled on my leash, but not as hard this time. "Come here, Sweeney, good girl."

"Not right here," Billy said, and pointed. "In the woods over there."

Nick said, "Why not here? People run here all the time. They'll be more likely to find her here."

*Find her? Find who?* Surely they weren't talking about me. I didn't need anyone to find me.

Billy and Nick yelled at each other for a moment, then Nick turned to me. He looked sad again. "Sweeney, we're leaving some food for you," he said.

"I just know someone's going to grab you up and take care of you. And . . . I'm really sorry things didn't work out with us."

*What's he doing?* I thought. *I thought we were going to play, but he's tying my leash to a tree. Hey! Hey, wait!*

I barked and barked, but Billy and Nick just turned away and kept walking!

I heard a slamming noise, and then Dad's car cranked up. "No! Please don't!" I barked at them. "I won't bark no more . . . or go to the bathroom on the floor, either! I'm sorry! Please come back!"

But they didn't come back. I barked and barked until I couldn't anymore, and then, I cried and cried. All I could hear was the sounds of cars passing by on the road.

After a long time, it started to get dark. Every once in a while, I heard funny noises. I started to cry again. *Is this a dream?* I kept thinking. All I wanted was to be back in Billy and Nick's room. At least there, I could hide under a bed when I was scared. Here, there wasn't anywhere I could hide. I couldn't even run.

Finally, I cried myself to sleep.

The next thing I heard was the sound of many cars zooming by. It took me a while to open my eyes. I didn't really want to. I just kept hoping it was a dream. Even a nightmare was better then this!

But after a while, I did open my eyes . . . and I started thinking. I turned to the tree, and saw that the leash was a little bit loose. *Maybe Nick didn't want to tie it too tight*, I thought. *Maybe he wanted me to escape!*

It took a while, but I was finally able to pull myself free!

But now, I really *was* homeless.

Here I was in the big world, alone and scared, and no one loved me. *If they'd just given me another chance! I just wanted to be loved and give love.*

*I had hope.*

But that was before. Now, I had nothing.

After a while, I started to feel a little better. Stronger. Hey, maybe I *was* just a puppy, but I was still smart! And I really wasn't alone. I realized that when I started to think about King and the other dogs. I was very far away from my neighborhood now, so I didn't think I'd ever see them again. But if King and his pack were homeless, there were probably lots of homeless animals out there. All I had to do was find them. Then, I wouldn't be alone! And even though I was scared, it still seemed better than living in the House of Misery. After a while, I began to think that maybe they did me a favor by leaving me here.

I heard a banging noise, and realized it was coming from the other side of a hill. I walked up the little hill to see a bunch of kids throwing rocks at a car. The car didn't look like Dad's. It didn't have any tires, and the windows were broken out. Maybe the car had been abandoned, too.

"Look," I heard one of the boys say. "There's a dog over there."

That made me feel good . . . until I heard another boy say, "Yeah, let's get that dog and throw rocks at it."

Then they all started running at me!

Unfortunately, Chihuahuas are little dogs, with short legs, and those kids ran faster than I could.

Behind me, I heard one of the kids yell as he ran into a tree stump. But the others kept after me. Then I heard one of the guys yelling, "Help me! Get me out of here! Joey! Tom! Pete! Help!"

I raced behind a tree to hide, then watched them trying to get their friend out of the hole. *Is this what I'm going to go through for the rest of my life?* I thought. *I'm so tired. Aren't there any nice people out there that like us dogs?*

And then, I thought of King. *If I run into him again, I'll stay with him and his pack. At least we'll be together.* But I didn't even know where I was. How in the world would I ever find King?

I was getting hungry now, and tired. I spotted a big rock with lots of green grass around it. I glanced at the boys; they were still busy trying to rescue their friend. I snuck over to my next hiding place.

After the longest time, it started to get dark, and I was scared again when I heard noises. But it was only birds flapping their wings. After a while, I saw the moon come out. Before now, I'd only seen it through a window. And the stars . . . they looked so beautiful! Now, it looked like there was no end to the sky.

I decided that, even if I spent the rest of my life alone, it was still better than the House of Misery. I just had to make some adjustments. Maybe, someone would even take me home with them, and love me. I think love is the most important and precious gift anyone can find. Maybe that's why Dad was so mean. Maybe he didn't have love, or know how to give love.

For a little while, I had hope. And I still felt that way when I fell asleep on my new bed made out of grass.

When I woke up, I could hear the birds whistling, and heard the wind as it moved the tree branches from side to side. The next thing I realized was how hungry I was. I looked around and sniffed at many things, but none of them seemed good to eat. So I started walking.

"Hello! Hello!"

I stopped walking just as the voice above me said, "Hey, over here."

I tensed, ready to run. I didn't want to encounter anyone else throwing rocks!

But this voice sounded kind when it said, "Hello, hello. I'm up here.

What's doing, little one?"

I turned around and saw . . . a squirrel!

"Up here," said the squirrel. "It's me. They call me Squeaky. What's doing?"

Finally, I relaxed. Sure, I'm a little dog. But I'm still a *lot* bigger than a squirrel. "Hi, Squeaky," I said. "My name's Sweeney."

"What are you doing all by yourself?"

"I . . . I'm homeless." I hated the sound of that word, but it was the truth.

"A little one like yourself shouldn't be out here by yourself," Squeaky said.

"That's why the homeless dogs stay in a pack."

As I looked and listened, Squeaky jumped from tree to tree.

"Wow, that looks cool!" I said. "I'm gonna give it a try."

Well, I tried. But when I tried to run up the tree, I fell flat on my back.

"Oops!" Squeaky said. "I don't think dogs can do that. But keep trying. You never know. Just be careful." She looked around. "Well, I gotta keep looking for nuts. It was nice meeting you, Sweeney. Hope to see you again." It felt good to have someone to talk to-especially someone so nice.

Then, I remembered there was some food back where Nick and Billy had left me. I started to walk away, hoping I could find it.

"Hey, Sweeney!"

I turned back around.

"Hey, if you ever come across a dog by the name of King and his pack, that's a bunch of cool dogs. Try to stay with them. They live on the west side of town." Squeaky pointed. "In that direction, I think. Just wanted to let you know that, Sweeney."

"Thanks, Squeaky," I said, then, "Hey, wait a minute. I know King and his pack. Seen them on my street! King gave me some good advice."

"That's King," Squeaky said. "Always looking to help. He hangs out with his friend, Prince. They're both alike. Just follow the road that leads you right into the city, Sweeney. I'm sure you'll find them. And be sure to tell them that Squeaky says hello!"

Then Squeaky went from one tree to another until she was gone, and I headed back in the direction of the road.

It's funny; I thought I didn't know where I was, but after I sniffed the ground a couple of times, I smelled something familiar. So by doing that, I soon found the road where they had left me, and the food was still there! I remembered what King told me . . . that often, he didn't know where his next meal would come from. So I ate until I couldn't eat any more, then started walking in the direction Squeaky had pointed to.

Cars beeped their horns at me, and I got scared again. One car stopped and a woman got out. "Come fellow, come on," she said. "Get in the car before you get hurt."

Fellow? Obviously, she couldn't tell I was a girl.

But after the last humans I encountered, I didn't trust *any* human. And besides, she didn't even know that I'm not a fellow, I'm a girl dog! I'm not going to jump in anyone's car if I don't know them. I might be small. But I'm not stupid.

I still followed the road, but now I stayed away from it as I walked. I saw another car pull over and stop. It was getting dark again, and I was behind a tree, so I didn't think anyone could see me.

The door opened. It was a woman, a much smaller woman than before.

And she had gray hair, so I knew she was old. And she had seen me after all. Yikes!

Just like the other woman, she said, "Come on, cutie, come on. Nobody's going to hurt you. Come, boy, everything's going to be all right."

Well, she wasn't any smarter than the last woman, but she seemed very nice. And by that point, I was getting hungry again.

*Maybe she'll be good to me,* I allowed myself to think. *Maybe she'll even love me. And maybe she has some food that she'll share.*

I moved closer to her, and she put her hand out. "Do you want to come home with me?" she asked.

I looked at her, and I suppose I must have looked awfully sad. She picked me up and sat me down next to her. In the front seat! I never got to ride in the front seat of a car before.

She didn't try to hurt me, just kept driving. After a while, I crawled over to her and laid my paw on her leg. She started rubbing my head, saying, "Everything's going to be all right."

And for the moment, I thought that maybe everything *was* going to be all right. *Maybe this is it for me,* I thought. *Maybe she's taking me home with her. That'll be nice. Maybe in time, we can learn to love each other.* I was so happy, I put my paws waaaay up and barked at her. She laughed. I licked her hand. She laughed again.

We drove for a long time, but finally she turned the car into the driveway of a big building, then opened her door and got out.

"Come on, girl," she said. "Come on, we're home."

*This is her house?* I thought. *Big building like this? Wow!*

I walked next to her. As we got closer to the building, I noticed a sign. The sign had a picture of a little boy hugging a dog and surrounded by cats. On the side, it read "ASPCA."

And then I remembered, and suddenly, I was terrified. Dad had also called it "the Humane Society," and said it was a place where bad dogs and cats went. And they never, ever came out!

I couldn't act like anything was wrong. But the first chance I got, I'm out of here!

But I couldn't help it. I started to cry. *I licked her face all over. I licked her so much, and she doesn't even want me?*

"What's the matter, cutie?" she said, and squatted down next to me. "Everything's going to be all right. Don't worry." Then she suddenly stood up. "Oops! I forgot my pocketbook in the car." She picked me up and walked back with me to the car. But when she put me down to open the door . . . *Zoom!* . . . I ran.

I could hear her say, "No, cutie, come back, come back!" But the more I heard her yell to come back, the faster I ran.

## CHAPTER 2

## Running Into

After a while, I got tired and had to slow down. I looked around me and saw houses, some big, long buildings, and a bigger building that had been painted red. I saw cows grazing in the field, and horses, too.

*Look like they're living well*, I thought. *Good for them.*

I sniffed around their food, but it wasn't anything I wanted to eat. So I started walking into some woods nearby.

The woods were big, and it took me a long time to get through them. As I emerged from them, I could hear dogs barking. I started walking slower, looking around me often. Soon, I came into what looked like a town. There were a lot of stores, and wonderful smells. The streets and everything looked so clean. I was just sure there was lots of good food here!

Then I heard the dogs barking again, closer now, and started to run. . . . . . .

. and ran right into a policeman!

*Nope, this isn't my day*, I thought.

The policeman didn't try to grab me, just stood there and smiled. "What do we have here? You're a small one. You shouldn't be out here by yourself. It's almost dark."

He reached out, but I was so afraid to move, I couldn't even run. He was huge-much bigger than Dad. But there was something about him that I liked. He had dark brown hair, and his eyes matched his hair. Brown eyes, just like mine. But that wasn't what I liked so much. It was the expression in his eyes and on his face.

Friendly and gentle, just like his smile. Just like the way he talked to me, too. It didn't take me long to realize that he would never, ever look at me mean, like Dad had done.

He felt of my neck, as if he was looking for something. "Uh, oh," he said after a moment. "No collar, no license." He gave me a curious look. "Are you a runaway? Whatever you are, you look good and healthy. Don't worry. We're going to take good care of you. Where I work at the Humane Society, they'll give you a nice bath, and get you something to eat. We might even find you a home. Many good people are looking for a Chihuahua like you. But tonight, you come home with me."

*So he's not a policeman, I guess. . . . Hey, wait a minute! Dad said the Humane Society is a bad place. But now, this guy's saying they'll give me a bath, and feed me too?*

I thought about the old lady that tried to take me inside the Humane Society. She was so nice. And Dad wasn't. Well, at least not much. And now this guy with the kind brown eyes is saying the Humane Society is a good place.

He kept talking, rubbing me behind the ears. That felt good. But I kept thinking. I had a big decision to make-whether I should run again, or go to the Humane Society.

I looked up. It was getting dark again, and now, I was starving. My belly was hitting my backbone, like Dad used to say.

*Well, he's going to take me to his house tonight, anyway*, I thought. *Maybe I can decide by tomorrow. If I don't like the idea by tomorrow, I'll just run away again.*

His house wasn't big, and it wasn't small. But to me at that moment, it looked just right. It was funny. Instead of taking me in the front door, he took me downstairs, into the basement. That scared me a little. But he gave me some food and water right away. And boy, was I hungry! After I ate, I had to kind of roll myself onto the blanket he'd fixed for me in the corner.

"Smallone, you'll stay here tonight," he said. "Sleep tight. I'm glad we ran into each other. Oh, and I forgot to tell you before . . . my name's Tom." He paused a moment, then said, "I would bring you upstairs, but my wife is allergic to dogs, cats and any other animals. She gets sick when she smells them. But it's warm and dry down here."

I wished I could talk. If I could, I'd tell him, "Hey, Tom, this blanket's a lot better than sleeping outside in the grass! At least nobody's going to throw rocks at me here, either."

But I couldn't talk, so I licked his hand instead.

He gave me a final ear rub-Nice!-and said goodnight.

As I lay on the bed he fixed for me, I tried not to think too much about tomorrow. But one thing I knew; I had to trust this fellow. He took me into his house, and fed me. Even though I can't talk, I think he understood my licks. And he hadn't yelled at me, even once. That said a lot.

*I hope Tom's not mad at me for not being more playful with him*, I thought, feeling sleepy. *And I hope I can stay here forever. I really like-"* And just like that, I fell asleep.

The next morning, as soon as I opened my eyes, I heard Tom coming down the stairs, and I quickly stood on my hind legs and showed my teeth.

"Good morning, Smallone," he said. "Did you sleep well? Hope so. Here's some food and water, then we'll get going. Give me about twenty minutes, okay?"

Again, I wished I could talk like humans can. I wanted to thank him. I wanted to tell him how much I loved him for taking care of me. For giving me hope in people. The hope that every human wasn't like Dad, and wasn't like those boys who tried to throw rocks at me. For not threatening me with a belt, or the Humane Society-

Oh, no. I forgot about that. And now, I had to decide.

It didn't take me long. Sure, *he* was all right, but I still didn't know about the Humane Society. I decided to run the first chance I got.

Or maybe not. I mean, maybe Dad was just saying that to scare me. He was always doing stuff like that. So far, I'd met two humans who acted like the Humane Society was a good place, and one who didn't. So Dad was outvoted-for now.

Even so, I was still nervous about it, and hoped I'd made the right decision.

Just as I was licking my dog bowl clean, I heard the door open.

"Smallone, are you finished? Come on, girl."

Tom bent over, and I ran and jumped right into his outstretched arms. I started licking his face, and he laughed. "Hey, Smallone, settle down. I hope you're gonna be as happy at the Humane Society as you look now."

As he spoke, we were walking toward the basement door, and a lady was walking toward us, a pretty lady with long, dark hair and blue eyes and white teeth with a loving smile that looked just like Tom's.

"Hi, honey," she said, "What do we have here?"

"Oh, it's just a little dog I'm going to bring to work with me today," Tom said.

The lady smiled. "Did you run after this one, too, or did it just jump right into your arms? Let me see her." She leaned close to me. "Oh, Tom, she's adorable! Ach-ooo!"

Tom smiled and pulled me away from her. "Go take your medicine, Columbia."

She sniffled, then said, "Oh, I'll be all right. She's just so cute! Maybe we could keep her. Maybe fix her a home here in the basement."

*I'll second that*, I barked, and wiggled and licked Tom's hand.

But Tom shook his head. "I'd love to, honey, but you know how you get with your allergies. And if we keep her down here, she'll be lonely while I'm at work. I'll get you some fish, okay?"

"Ha, ha, very funny." Columbia looked at me, and her eyes were . . . I guess you'd call them wistful. Like she was happy and sad at the same time.

"What are you calling her, Tom?" "Smallone."

Columbia nodded. "Great name, and a small one she is." She looked at me, and there was that wistful look again. "Oh, Smallone, I wish I could keep you. But I just know you'll like it at the Humane Society."

Okay, that was three votes, and all from people who are nice *all* of the time. Now, I have a little hope!

For the second time in my life, I got to sit in the front seat, right next to Tom. As he drove, he told me about the Humane Society. When he finished, he said, "Our shelter puts on a show-a television show. We call it *Pets for Adoption*. People from all over watch it. If they're looking for a pet to adopt, they come to the Humane Society and take their pick."

He reached down and rubbed me behind the ears again. Heaven! Then he told me some more stuff.

"But anyone who wants a pet has to be interviewed first by Dr. Casey. He's the vet, and he kind of runs things. There's Gail, Terry and Lisa, too. They work at the reception. They set up appointments and tests. Sometimes Lisa does interviews, too." He gave me a smile. "Lisa's tough. If they don't pass the interview, they get denied for adoption. That means they can't get a pet. Sometimes when they get denied, they put a fuss. That's where I come in. I'm the security guard. I keep it nice and quiet. There's also Victor. He helps the doc and takes care of the cages. Johnny, he's the dogcatcher. George is also a catcher. He and Johnny alternate driving. . . ."

What Tom was saying sounded good, but I still felt nervous. *What if nobody wants to adopt me? Will they let me stay? When I get old, will they drive me to the woods and leave me there?*

I thought about running away again. Because once I was behind those big doors at the Humane Society, there was no telling what might happen.

"We're here," Tom said, and I felt the car slow, then stop.

He got out and held out his arms. I took a deep breath and looked at the opening between him and the door. I could make it through there.

"Come on, Smallone," he repeated.

I took a deep breath, and made my decision. I started running . . . and hopped right into his arms.

As we walked up to the Humane Society doors, I licked his face, and he laughed.

"Don't worry, Smallone, I'll come up and see you every day."

I think if you have love, you have the most precious gift in the world. And that's what I felt for Tom right now.

I could see the writing on the door as Tom and I entered the building. It read,

"Humane Society of Connecticut, you'll find your love pet here."

*Love*, I thought. And I felt good. And then I realized that feeling good was happening more and more.

We entered this big room, where two girls were talking on the phone and looking kind of busy. One of the girls hung up the phone and said, "Hi, Tom.

What'cha got?"

"Lisa, good morning."

Oh, so this was Lisa. She was a big pretty girl, with long brown hair and big brown eyes.

"What do we have here?" she said. "He's so cute!" "He's a she, Lisa."

"So what's her name?"

Tom was quiet a moment, then said, "I don't know. I've been calling her Smallone."

Lisa smiled and said, "Smallone she is. I'll be right back." After she left, Tom said, "There's Gail and Terry, Smallone." Terry, a very short woman with dark hair, had just walked out from a hallway behind the counter, and smiled at me.

Now, Gail was off the phone, and said, "Where did you find her?"

"She found me. I wanted to keep her, but you know . . . Columbia's allergies. I told her I'd get her some fish."

Everyone laughed, then Tom said, "But I know she'll be a great pet for someone. And I'd like to meet the one who adopts her."

Lisa nodded. "I know what you mean." She reached out and pushed some kind of button. "Go on back and let Dr. Casey check her out."

As we were walking down the hall, I started to get nervous again. Sure, the people seemed nice, and the place was clean. But I didn't see any other dogs around.

Just then, we approached a door that read "A NEW BEGINNING." I liked that. It sounded like . . . hope.

I guess Tom could feel that I was shaking a little. He said, "Smallone, you know why there's a new beginning on the doctor's door? Ninety-five percent of the dogs he looks at, they get better. The other five percent that come here are in bad shape, so there really isn't anything he can do for them. But you? You're in great shape!"

You think Tom can read minds? I don't know why he said that to me, but I definitely needed to hear it just then. So I listened extra- close when he continued.

"Sometimes, an animal is in so much pain and misery, the best thing to do is to let them go into the animal kingdom. So they can be free. It's sad, but if I was very sick, that's how I'd want to go. In peace, and no suffering."

You know, that didn't sound too bad. But, from what Tom said, I wouldn't have to worry about that for a long time.

## CHAPTER 3

# Life At The Humane Society, & Hope

Tom knocked on the door, and a man's voice answered. Tom opened the door and we walked in.

"Hi, Tom, what do we have here?" The man was standing next to a Labrador retriever on a tall table. And hey, the dog looked happy! Things were looking up!

"She found me," Tom replied. "Her name is Smallone. She jumped right into my arms."

Well, that wasn't *exactly* like I remembered it-actually, I ran right into him! But that's okay.

"Could you check her out for me, Doc?" Tom said. "You're not keeping this one?"

"I'd like to. But you know Columbia-"

Dr. Casey nodded. "Yes, allergies. I remember now. Give me about a half an hour."

Tom said, "Sure, Doc. Thanks for everything. See you in about a halfhour."

A half-hour later, Tom left me with the doctor. I didn't like it. Dr. Casey listened to my heart, checked my eyes. *What's this? NO!* I barked at the needle.

"Don't worry, Smallness . . . I mean, Smallone!" Dr. Casey said. "I just want to check your blood. Let's check your weight now." Okay, that wasn't too bad.

"You're in great shape," he said. "You won't last long here, that's for sure. Anybody would love to have a dog like you. I'll call Tom to take you to the shelter. You'll meet a lot of friends there."

For some reason, it felt like things were getting better for me. And I didn't think this was the end of the dusty road I had to look forward to. Things would work out. I was just sure of it.

Soon, Tom came to get me, and we walked down a long hallway.

"Smallone, that wasn't too bad, was it?"

I wanted to tell him it wasn't too bad at all, so I licked his hand. At the end of the hall, Tom opened a door and walked into a room. There were all kinds of things happening in there, and all kinds of animals! Three barking dogs. Two cats. A couple of birds, even. And best of all, a great big window where I could see trees and sunshine!

But then, something happened that I didn't like too much. Tom opened the door of a cage and put me in there, and the cage was right next to the cages of three big dogs!

A minute later, the door opened kind of fast, and in came one of the catchers with a dog, a cat and . . . a chicken!

*A chicken?* I thought. *What?*

The chicken didn't look very well. She looked bad, if you ask me.

Dr. Casey came in and said, "Hello, Johnny, what do we have here?"

"Doc, I found the dog in the park. The cat down by the tracks. The chicken was by the horse stables through the woods, and she doesn't look too good.

Could you have a look at her?"

"Sure, Johnny, sit her over here."

Johnny sat her on a table, then said, "I'll get a few things, and be right back."

While he was gone, I was thinking. *So this is Johnny. He seems like a nice guy.*

Johnny came back in and looked at me. "What brings a cute dog like you over here?"

"Tom found her last night," Dr. Casey said, and gave a knowing smile. "He said she ran right into his arms. She's in great shape." "What are you calling her?" Johnny said.

"Smallone. Tom wanted to keep her, but Columbia has allergies."

Johnny nodded. "Yeah, I remember. But I'm sure Smallone will find a home soon."

I could hear the sound of jangling keys, and Tom came into the room and walked over to me, opened the cage door, and I jumped right into his arms.

I watched Dr. Casey as he examined her, gave her some medicine, and fixed a few cuts she had. Next thing I heard was the chicken going "Bock, bock!"-and it flapped its wings and jumped off the table!

The dogs started barking and the cats were meowing and Johnny was trying to catch the chicken, with no luck. Tom put me back in the cage and helped Johnny catch it.

Dr. Casey checked the bandages he'd just put on the chicken, then said, "She'll be all right. Tom, put her in the cage. In a couple of days, we can take her back to the stables."

The more I see how things, are done here, the more I like what I see. And I'm beginning to like it here more and more. They even take good care of chickens!

Gail and Terry came in and said, "Hi, Johnny. Where's Smallone?"
"Over there."

Uh, oh, they were coming my way!

But Terry started petting my head, and it felt good. "Hi, cutie, hope you're feeling good." Definitely!

Then Gail, a tall, thin girl with blonde hair, started talking to me. "Smallone, sometimes we put on a show. It's called *Pets for Adoption*. Would you like to be in it next time? You're so cute, I wish I could take you home myself."

It was a great day. Terry, Gail, Johnny, Tom and Dr. Casey were in and out of the room all day. But eventually, things got kind of quiet. After a while, the only one there was Johnny. And oh, all the animals too. It had been so busy, I hadn't met them yet.

Tom came in, picked me up, kissed me on the head and said goodnight. I felt great. Like I never felt before. That was a feeling I wanted to have a little more often. Tom was the best man I ever met.

That night, someone named Victor came in with Johnny, and began cleaning.

He took me out of the cage and said, "Wait right here, Smallone, while I take care of your cage."

Johnny cleaned the tables, chairs and mirrors. After a while, Victor came over to me and said, "Smallone, your house awaits you."

When he put me in the cage, I went, "Oh, wow!" He'd fixed it up with a fluffy blanket! I laid down on it, and Victor said, "Goodnight."

Just as he said that, I heard a ringing noise, and Johnny said, "That's George. I'll let him in."

I lay in my cage, feeling good knowing there's people like the people here. People that liked us-dogs, cats, and all kinds of animals.

Soon, it was lights out-all except one that Johnny left on in the room. Just before he left, he said, "When we put on the show, I'm sure all of you are going to go. Love all of you. Goodnight."

I barked, stood on my hind legs and showed my teeth. Johnny came back and said, "What is it, Smallone? What is it? You have water, and a nice blanket."

I reached through the cage door and licked his hand.

He smiled. "Oh, you just wanted to say goodnight. Right?"

"Ruff!"

He laughed. "I love you too, Smallone."

Then he rubbed my head and left.

It was a great feeling that he understood me. I barked all the time in the House of Misery, but nobody ever acted like they knew what I was talking about. But Tom did, and Johnny too! I really liked this place. And I knew what love really was now. I loved everyone here. Well, I wasn't so sure about the chicken yet. But at least it wasn't squawking and flapping around now, just sitting in the cage, and appeared to be asleep.

And come to think of it, I wasn't so sure about my new roommates, either.

I turned and looked at the cage next to me. The dogs in there just looked back.

After a minute, the black dog said, "You think you're going to get put on one show, and you'll get adopted? I don't *think* so." "Ah, what do you mean by that?" I said.

"I *mean*, don't think you're going to get put on one of those shows and say „Adios, amigo.' I've been on a bunch of them, and look at me . . . I'm still sitting in this cage!" The black dog peered at me. I'm pretty sure he was a Black Lab. His look wasn't friendly, or unfriendly, just kind of suspicious. "By the way, what's your name, and what kind of dog are you?"

I thought a minute. "I'm a Chihuahua. And well, my name was Sweeney before, but they've been calling me Smallone." "Smallone? Ha! What kind of name is *that*?"

"That's what Tom and Columbia started calling me. So everyone calls me that. What are they calling you?"

"They call me by my name. Blackie. Blackie is my *name*."

Suddenly, I was a little nervous. "Blackie you are," I said. "Nice to meet you, Blackie. So, they didn't give you that name?"

Blackie made a disgusted snuffling. "No, Smallone. My owners gave it to me."

"You had a home, Blackie?"

"Yes, I did, Smallone. And a family." "Yeah? Why are you here?"

Blackie placed his head on his paws, and didn't look at me anymore. But he did answer. "Well, we had a fire in the apartment we live in. Once they get another apartment or a house, they're going to come and take me home."

"Hey, Blackie, that's great. I'm happy for you."

"Yeah, that's what he's telling himself." A big, white-haired dog with watery eyes jumped in. His long hair made him look kind of like a collie mixed with a retriever. "It's been how long, Blackie?" the white-haired dog said. "Two, three months?"

Blackie lifted his head and glared at the dog. "Well, I'm sure they didn't get settled yet, Prince."

I decided to butt in. You know, kind of try to break the tension. I turned to the third dog, who hadn't said anything yet. "So, what's your name?"

"I'm Lady. And please forgive us for not welcoming you to the Humane Society yet. It's so busy in the daytime here, we barely get a word in edgewise." She extended a paw. "But allow me to officially welcome you.

You met Blackie, I'm Lady, and that's Prince who sounds so discouraged."

Prince nodded. "Hi, Smallone."

"Hi, Prince," I said, and turned back to Lady. "So how long have you been here, Lady?"

"Well, I've been here for six months, and Prince been here for six months."

"Why so long?"

Lady was quiet for a moment, then said, "Well, not everybody wants old dogs."

But, you dogs aren't old," I said.

"Compared to puppies like you, we are. But, we haven't given up hope yet.

Dr. Casey told us there is a need for all types and ages of dogs." "Have you guys been on that pet adoption show yet?" Lady shook her head.

"Why not?"

She sighed. "Well, Blackie and I decided that if they want us, they'll come and get us."

Now I was really confused. "But if they don't see you, they won't know you're here."

Prince spoke up. "Smallone has a point there, Lady. I mean, I know you're shy and all, but . . . I think the next time Terry asks us if we want to be on the show, you should act excited. Then you'll get on the show."

Lady gave a sigh. "Well, that's up to you, Prince. But I just think it's trashy to be on television."

"Well, I don't need to be on some adoption show," Blackie said. "I have a family, and they're coming to get me!"

Lady looked at him, but didn't say anything, just glanced at me and gave a sympathetic whimper.

"I do the show all the time," Prince said. "And I'm just sure that, someday, a family will adopt me."

Lady looked at Blackie for a while, and then said, "Blackie, maybe your family is just distracted. You know . . . the fire, and finding a new place to live and all. Maybe if they know you're going to be on the show, it will remind them that they need to come and get you."

Blackie thought a moment. "Well, maybe." Then he was quiet for a long time, and his eyes were so sad, I wanted to lick his face.

Finally, he said, "You know, sometimes I think they've forgotten about me.

Sometimes . . . I think they're not going to come."

"Have faith in people," I told him. "There are some nice people out there. I met at least three of them, just today. Did they treat you good? Your family, I mean."

Blackie nodded. "Yes they did, all the time."

"Don't worry then, Blackie. They'll be here for you."

Blackie looked at me with hope in his eyes. "You think so, Smallone?"

"Yes, I do. If they showed you that much love, like you said, they probably didn't get settled yet. You'll be fine, Blackie."

"Thanks, Smallone." He looked from one to the other, and then back to me.

"I'm sure there's a place for all of us."

I nodded, then said to Lady, "Lady, what about you? Did you have love and happiness out there? A nice family?"

"Yes, I did Smallone. Until my owner, PaPo, got sick. His wife, Elsey, couldn't take care of me anymore." She sighed. "It was just as well. She rarely took me out, and it seemed to bother her when she had to feed me." She gave a shake of her head, then said, "But enough about me. Tell us, Smallone, was it nice for you out there? When you lived with your family?"

Gosh, I was hoping I'd never have to think about that again. But these guys had been straight with me so far, and I owed Lady an answer. "Well, guys, you're not going to like this. „Cause I call that house I came from the House of Misery. That's what it was. They used to chase me with a belt, they rarely gave me anything to eat, and I was always afraid." "Oh, how awful, Smallone!" Lady said.

"So what did you do? Run away?" Prince said. "Is that how you ended up here?"

"Oh, no!" I replied. "I used to think about it, though. Especially after I met this pack from the West Side."

"Don't tell me," Lady said. "The leader was King. Right?" That surprised me. "You know King, Lady?"

She shrugged. "Who doesn't?" She looked at Prince, and he nodded.

"He made me feel good," I told them. "Until I met him, I thought I was alone, feeling the way I did."

"King's pack is the toughest and coolest pack on the West Side," Prince said. "Every now and then, I would hang out with King. That's how I met King. He's an older dog, like me, but really tough."

Lady said, "Smallone, what brought you here?" "Well, one day the boys and Dad took me for a ride." "Oh, no, not the car ride."

I looked at Prince, confused. And then it hit me: Maybe that was the way a lot of dog owners got rid of their pets when they didn't want them anymore. I nodded. "Yeah, Prince. The car ride.

But when he said that, I got so excited and happy, I started to feel bad that I was thinking about running away. But the next day, they took me for the ride, and tied me to a tree. But I pulled myself free from it. Some boys chased me, but I was able to run away. And then I met a friend." "You met someone?" Lady said.

"Yes, I did. A squirrel. Her name was Squeaky. So that was good. And would you believe that Squeaky knows King?" "*Everyone* knows King," Lady said.

"Go on," Blackie said. "Lady, let her finish."

"I started walking on the road, and this sweet old lady picked me up. I thought she was taking me to her house, but she took me to this place that has a dog with a boy hugging it chipped out in stone."

"Oh, that's the ASPCA," Prince said. "What's that?" I asked.

"It's just like this place. They take care of us."

"Hey, that's a good thing," I said. "But I didn't know that then. When . . . When I was still in the House of Misery, Dad told me that it was a terrible place. So the first chance I got, I ran away."

Lady shook her head. "Sounds so typical. It's hard to believe, but many pet owners threaten their pets by saying things like that." Maybe Dad wasn't so rare, after all. "Well, after running away from her, I ran right into Tom. Tom and his wife took good care of me last night. And now, here I am with you guys. I love Tom and his wife." I gave them a long look. "And I love you too."

Lady smiled and chuckled. "We love you, too, Smallone." "That's right, Smallone," Blackie said. "That goes for all of us. Right, guys?"

All I heard after that was, "Ruff! Ruff! Ruff!" and "Meoooow!" Lady turned back to me and said, "See, Smallone? Even the cats are with you."

I tell you, after that, I didn't care about anything that had happened to me before now. Even if I never found a family, I already had all the family a dog needs!

"Smallone?" "Yes, Lady?"

"Someone special is going to adopt you, and soon. I'm just sure of it."

"Well, I hope not too soon, „cause you guys are great." "Anyway, Smallone, it might take a few weeks before we go on the network. To do the adoption show." "Why's that, Lady?"

"It takes money. I heard Dr. Casey and Tom talking about it. It costs a lot of money. Everything costs a lot of money."

For the next few minutes, Lady, Blackie and Prince talked about how the Humane Society was operated on something called "donations," and they always had to wait until there were enough of those donations to pay the local television station to air the adoption show. All of it was interesting, but I had a hard time following them, because it had been a long day.

"Guys, Blackie, Prince, Lady . . . I'm getting kind of tired now." Lady nodded. "I understand, Smallone. When I was a puppy, I slept almost all the time. You get some rest, and we'll see you in the morning."

"Okay, Lady," I said. "Goodnight, sleep tight. That's what Nick used to say."

And I rolled into my fluffy blanket, and that's the last thing I remembered.

# CHAPTER 4

# Getting To Know The Gang

Over the next couple of days, I came to understand that life in the Humane Society was nice enough, but a little confining. Oh, we got to go outside. But when it was time to go back in, I always felt a little sad, and took one last look at the sky, the singing birds and the trees blowing in the wind. And although I didn't get to talk to the cats much, I found out two of their names. One was Beauty; she was all black, and very pretty. The other one, they called Minsk. Minsk looked like an alley cat, with green eyes and striped fur.

One night, Lady and Blackie and I got to talking. Prince had played extra hard while we were outside, and was already sound asleep.

"Lady, there's something that I've never gotten the nerve to ask Prince," I said.

She just gave me a curious look, and I said. "I mean, Prince is a handsome dog. Smart, too. I can't understand why nice dogs like that wind up in places like this."

Lady glanced over at Prince; he was still sleeping. Then she turned her head back to me. "Well, Smallone, Prince came from a nice, well-to-do family."

"So, what happened?"

She shook her head. "Very sad. The family that Prince lived with had a baby. And the baby was always sick, and the doctor said it was because of Prince. So, hoping the baby would get better, they brought Prince here."

*Maybe the baby had allergies, too,* I thought, then asked Blackie, "So did the baby get better?"

Blackie shook his head, very sad. "No, Smallone. The baby died last month. The baby had a heart disease. A very rare one. I heard the staff talking about it. So it wasn't because of Prince."

"So why don't the family take him back?"

"Well, I heard the girls in the office talking. They were saying something like the reason the family had Prince was because of the baby, and being that the baby is no longer here, it would only being bad memories."

"Pardon me for saying this," I said, "but that sucks. Prince didn't do anything wrong!"

Blackie nodded, and Lady said, "Well, you know how it goes, Smallone. Dogs like King don't depend on people, but we do."

I nodded. "But we have feelings too. Is that the reason Prince has watery eyes?"

"Yes. It's because he cries himself to sleep every night."

As Blackie was telling me that, I couldn't help it; I started to shed tears for him, too. "Oh, Blackie, we have to do something for him."

"What could we do, Smallone?" "What? I don't know."

"Over here, over here." When I heard the noise from far away, I jumped.

"It's the cats, Smallone."

I looked over to see Beauty and Minsk hanging on the bars of their cage.

Beauty's fur was so shiny, I could see it gleaming in the dim light.

"The show, Smallone!" Minsk said, and her green eyes flashed.

"What do you mean, the show?"

"I mean, why don't we all put on a nice show the next time they have enough donations to have the adoption show?"

"What are you taking about?" Blackie said, sounding mad. "Why don't you just go to sleep?"

"No, Blackie, Minsk has a point," Lady said. "Yes, that's a good idea, Minsk."

"Thank you," Minsk said, then turned back to look at me. "Smallone, that's the idea with that adoption show, right? To get adopted. So why don't we try? When the show comes on, we'll all just give „em a show! I mean, what else are we going to do . . . just stay here and wait to die? I know there's a lot of fun out there. We just haven't found it yet."

"Yes," Beauty said. "There are surely people out there that could love us and take care of us. We could be their friends, and watch their house, and love them."

Minsk looked at me, surprise on her kitty face. "Beauty has never talked that way before, Smallone. You've only been here a few days, and you have the whole place happier."

Hearing that made me so happy, I put my paws up and barked! Which, since Minsk was a cat, scared her-she fell off the cage bars.

"Oh, sorry about that, Minsk. I forgot you're a cat."

"That's okay, Smallone. You're so small, sometimes I forget you're a dog."

"Well, I *never* forget I'm a dog."

Hearing that, we all jumped and turned around. Prince was awake, rubbing his eyes.

"Prince, I thought you were asleep," Lady said. "Did we awaken you?"

"Oh, that's all right," Prince replied. "But I heard what Minsk said. I think she's right. If we all work together, we'll be able to put on a great show."

"Except me," Blackie said. "I don't need to, because my family-"

"Blackie," Minsk said, "even if your family comes back to get you, this is a way you can help us. Won't you at least think about it?"

After a moment, Blackie growled softly. "Okay, I'll think about it. But no promises!"

Minsk looked at me with her green eyes. "Okay, Smallone, what are we going to do when we're on TV?"

I thought a moment. "Hummm. I don't know." "Well, maybe I could sing and dance," Lady said. I turned to her, surprised.

"Well, I used to know how," she said. "Perhaps I could remember."

I shrugged and said, "Sure. Anything and everything you like. But, what could I do?"

"Lady, that's great," Minsk butted in. "I can dance, too, and Beauty could sing."

"Well, I'm like Smallone," Prince said. "I don't know what I could do."

Trying to encourage him, I said, "Maybe you won't have to do anything,

Prince. I'm sure Johnny and Victor will brush your fur right before the show.

And it will look just like gold."

"Well, maybe I could pace around. I'm pretty good at that," Prince said. "Or maybe even run in a circle." He looked around the cage. "Not much room to practice here, but maybe I can practice while I'm outside."

"Okay," I said. "You'll do that." I looked around the room. "Look at all the talent we have here. There's nothing we can't do. And it'll be fun."

"So, Smallone," Lady said. "Any ideas about what you can do?" I thought long and hard, then said, "I'll jump." She gave me a skeptical look, and I explained. "I'm so small, I have to jump a lot . . . you know, to reach chairs, windows, things like that." I glanced at the window, right next to my cage. "I could jump right out of that window if I wanted."

Lady gave me a funny look. "I don't mean to be impolite, but . . . as small as you are, you could make the window?" "Yes!" I said.

"Yeah, right," Blackie said, and snickered.

"You don't believe I can jump that high? Okay, watch."

It went pretty well, except that I forgot about the cage's ceiling, and smacked against it. It took a while for the laughter to calm down. Even the chicken cackled while I rubbed my sore head against my blanket.

"Wow, you almost made it," Lady said, trying to soothe my embarrassment.

"I'll give another try," I said. (Hey, Chihuahuas are famous for their selfconfidence!) Lady put her paw out. "Maybe you should wait until we're outside."

I glanced at the ceiling, and then back down. "Yeah, I guess you're right."

Lady smiled. "All right, Smallone. But I'm very impressed by how high you jumped." She glanced at the window. "If that window was open, you could leave here if you really wanted to, couldn't you?"

"Yeah, I guess. But what for? To be running all my life? I used to think that would be nice, but I'm not so sure anymore. I feel good that I ran into Tom, and he brought me here to be with you guys. You guys are great."

"No, Smallone, *you* are," Lady said. "You've given us a great idea."

Lady, Blackie, Prince, Minsk and Beauty all stood up and barked, meowed and clapped. And I definitely had hope that we would all find families someday.

The next day was busy. I practiced my jumping, Prince practiced pacing around, and Lady did a remarkable job of singing and dancing, too. Blackie spent most of the time lying on the grass, watching us with a scowl. But I didn't mind.

That night after supper, we were all tired, but so excited, we talked a while, making plans for the show.

"Okay, guys, look. . . . It's really getting late. Let's get some sleep."

Lady yawned. "Oh, dear, you're right. All that singing and dancing made me tired. I think we could all do with a night's sleep, don't you?"

Soon, the whole room was filled with only the sounds of sleep, and the occasional clucking of our resident chicken.

I heard someone coming and opened my eyes. *Oh, it's Dr. Casey. And hey, what's that he's got in his arms?*

"Hi Smallone did you sleep well?" he said. "You want go out to the yard?" He looked around the room, then turned back to me. "Hummm. There are no open cages right now, but you've got lots of room in yours. So I'll put this little one in with you for now." He laid what looked like a little ball of fuzz in my cage, but I was so excited about going outside, I kind of ignored it.

When he took me outside, I realized this just wasn't any visit- this was a day when new owners got acquainted with us pets. But, not me today. So I spent the time practicing with Lady, Prince and the cats.

As he was returning me to the cage, he stopped at the front desk. Gail and Terry were talking to a man who looked kind of upset.

"Dr. Casey," Gail said with a funny look on her face, "this is Mr. Luigi. And he wants to know if anyone brought in his chicken."
"Yes," Mr. Luigi said in a heavy accent. "My chicken is nowhere to be found. She would never wander off."

"Was she by the railroad tracks?" Terry asked. "If she was, she could get hurt, Mr. Luigi. That's not a good place for her. And why was she loose, anyway?"

"She made a hole by the fence and went under the fence!" Mr. Luigi said.

Terry scowled. "Come on, Mr. Luigi. Do you mean to tell me that your chicken was able to dig a hole?"

Mr. Luigi nodded. "Yes, she must have. And if I find her, you know what I'm going to do? I'm going to put concrete under the fence. Then she won't get out."

Terry went to the back room, and came back a moment later holding the chicken. Her face was serious, and her next words matched her expression. "Well, Mr. Luigi, you have to do something, because if she gets out again and we find her . . . Well, it's the responsibility of every pet owner to keep their pet safe. Do you feed the chicken good, Mr. Luigi?"

Mr. Luigi smiled. "Do I feed the chicken good? Look how fat she is! That's why I can't figure out how she made it under the fence. I could see her head making it, but that fat belly beats me. But that's my chicken, sure enough."

He leaned over and began talking like a baby. "You want to come home with Papa?" He made a few soft clucking noises at her, then turned back to Terry and Gail. "You see, Miss Terry and Gail? She wants to come home."

Gail sighed. "Okay, Mr. Luigi, let's see some ID, and sign here. Then you can go. And please, Mr. Luigi, make sure she doesn't get out again."

"Sure, I'll fix it right away," he said. "My family is in construction. I get a good price on concrete." Terry handed the chicken to Mr. Luigi, and he said,

"Girls, thank you."

Gail and Terry didn't look too happy about giving the chicken back.

After Mr. Luigi left, the phone rang, and Terry picked it up. She listened a moment, then said, "Sure, let's set up a time, When do you want to come?

Tomorrow at two? Sounds good. See you guys then."

## ROCKET & THE CONSTRUCTION WORKER

When she hung up, she turned to Gail and said, "Gail, it's the camera crew.

They're coming out tomorrow."

*Uh, oh,* I thought. *I'm nowhere close to being ready for the show!*

Then Terry said, "They're just coming to check out the scene . . . you know, to get a better idea. They did that last month, too." "Yeah, I know,"

Gail said. "Did they say when the show will be taped?"

"Two weeks from tomorrow." I was so relieved, I barked.

"Oh," Dr. Casey said to me. "I guess I'd better get you back to your cage for now, Smallone." The puppy was still in there, but I never minded having a roommate, especially a little one. This time, I took a closer look. The puppy was so little, it was hard to tell, but I thought it must be a Lab. She was golden, with a little white tip on her tail. Basically, she was adorable. I started to smell her, and she went "Ruff!", "Ruff!" But her bark was high-pitched, and so cute that I lay down next to her and she laid her head down on my stomach.

Everyone was so excited when I told them we had two weeks before our big show. Even Minsk and Beauty acted thrilled, and I didn't think cats could do that.

The film crew's visit happened when I was asleep, so I missed it. But that didn't stop our eagerness. The news of the show spread through the Humane Society like raindrops coming down on a rainy day. We all practiced hard, and Prince paced and turned around in circles until he got so dizzy, he had to lie down. If you asked me, we were all good. Minsk and Beauty didn't really practice anything. But they were cats, so I guess they had their own ideas about how to impress people. And the Lab puppy didn't practice anything but being a puppy. And Blackie? Well, he pretty much just wandered around and didn't say much . . . until the morning before the show. "Smallone?"

I turned to see Blackie in his cage, and he looked really sad.

"Yes, Blackie?"

"What am I going to do?"

I couldn't believe what I just heard. "In . . . In the show, you mean?" He nodded.

"Blackie, that's great. You-"

"But I don't know what I'll do," he said. "You're going to jump, Prince is going to run in circles, and Lady will sing and dance. But what will I do?"

"What do you like to do?" I asked him."

He shrugged. "I like to eat, play, sleep, and go for walks."

"Not regular stuff," I said. "*Special* stuff. Do you like to sing, hop, or dance?"

His face brightened a bit. "Yeah, Smallone, I like to dance." He turned to Lady and said, "Remember when we danced?"

Lady nodded. "We sure did have fun, Blackie. And you were great." "Then that's it," I said. "You and Lady dance."

Blackie shook his head. "Oh, no, Smallone. I wasn't that good at it." "Come on, give it a try," I said.

"Okay, okay."

"Maybe we'll all be adopted," I said. "Let's keep the faith."

Lady looked confused. "Faith, Smallone? What's that?"

"It means confidence, Lady. Confidence in yourself."

She nodded. "Okay, let's give our best, and keep the faith."

The staff was getting ready to call it a day. Johnny came in to say goodnight, and Tom did, too. It was really good to see him-especially when he scratched me behind the ears, like he'd done before.

"Goodnight, Smallone," he said, and smiled at my roommate. "I heard you have a little friend."

Someone from the office called out, "Hey, Tom, we're leaving now!"

He smiled at me and said, "Hey, I guess I'll see you guys tomorrow. People from all over will see you and all your friends. This is a good chance to lead all of you to a happy family and a beautiful home you'll love, Smallone." He kissed me on the head, said goodbye, and he was gone.

As he was leaving, a thought came over me of joy. I felt sad for King and the others, and wished that maybe they will be as lucky as me to meet a nice man like Tom.

I thought everyone had left, but I was wrong. Johnny stuck his head in. "I just wanted to tell everyone that whatever you do tomorrow, do it good. If you guys can't think of anything to do, just look pretty, and maybe you'll all find nice families. I'll see everyone in the morning. Goodnight."

Some time passed by, and I said, "Blackie and Lady are going to dance together. Minsk and Beauty, they're going to . . . well, maybe dance and meow. Prince is going to be Prince. I'll jump. The little Lab is going to just sit there looking pretty. And guys, we'll all shine like stars. And I just know there's good people out looking for some guys like us to hang on to."

Lady had tears running down her face. "Oh, Smallone, I love you. I love all of you. Who knows? We could be blessed, and be adopted by good people. Smallone, thank you for inspiring us to do well. You're the best, Smallone."

In my dream, I was in a big field, looking up at the stars. This man was rubbing my head as we gazed at them. I felt great. That's what I rememberhow good I felt. And then, I heard a noise. *Must be windy*, I thought in my dream.

As I opened my eyes, I heard keys going into the lock to the door, and saw it swing slowly open. It was George, and he had a dog with him. It was daylight, but it was still pretty dark, so I couldn't see the dog very well. I blinked, and saw that it looked like a German Shepherd. I started missing King.

"Hello," George said softly. "I hope it's not too late to enter one more in the show."

*Wait a minute*, I thought, *that looks like King. Hey, it* is *King!*

## CHAPTER 5

## King, And Showtime!

I couldn't help myself. I started barking. "Hey, everybody! Wake up! It's King!" I turned to King and barked, "King, how you been?"

"Doing all right, Sweeney," he barked. "I thought about you a lot, and I was worried."

"Hey, it's all right King. I'm here with my friends! And now you're here, so I'm with *all* my friends!"

I'll admit that we were being pretty noisy, so it took a while before we noticed George waving his hands in the air. We settled down long enough for him to say, "Whew! I guess all you guys either know each other, or really like each other. But I shouldn't be surprised, because King's been around a while."

George started to put King in the big cage, the one Mr. Luigi's chicken had occupied. Then he turned to me. "Smallone, this new fella's kind of old.

Could you help out with him?"

I barked and put my paws in the air.

George smiled and nodded. "Well, I know he's in good hands now."

Lady put her paw in the air and said, "Hello, King. It's good to see you again. You've come at a good time. We're going to be in a show first thing in the morning. Would you like to be in it with us?" King's brow furrowed and he looked at me.

"Oh, King, it's great," I said. "It's for adoption. People from all over will be watching. You want to be in it with us?"

King tensed. "Oh, no I don't! Nobody's going to adopt me. And even if I *did* want to be adopted, nobody wants an old dog like me." "That's crazy,

King," I said. "You're a great dog."

"You barely know me, Sweeney!"

"For one thing," I said, "I know you well enough to respect you. And for another thing, it's not Sweeney any more. Call me Smallone."

"Smallone?"

"Yes. That's my new name, and I like it. „Sweeney' was when I lived in the House of Misery. And I'm free of that now."

"Yeah, Smallone, I know all about it. We saw them come back without you." King grinned, then said, "You should have seen Toby, one of my gang. As soon as that mean old man and the two boys came back without you, she figured out what happened, and started barking at them and growling. The old man said, „Get out of here!' and started yelling at us. But Toby just kept barking until he ran all the way into his house!"

I couldn't help it-I had to laugh at the image of mean old Dad actually getting scared for once. But then, I was sad. "Yes, he *is* a very mean man," I said. "People like that shouldn't have pets."

King nodded. "We kind of knew what you were going through in that house. I was hoping, the next time I saw you outside, to talk you into running away with us. . . . We were afraid of what they might do to you."

"I was too," I said. "But it doesn't matter now. I'm happy, and I love these guys." I lifted my paw and swept it all around the room, then turned back to King. "But I'm so glad I got to see you again, King. I thought about you a lot."

"Me, too." He hunkered down in the cage and settled his head onto his paws. "So, you have a show?"

"Yep. And I really wish you'd think about-"

"Smallone, I know about the show. Remember? I've been here before. But I'd be wasting my time. Nobody's gonna want me."

I rested my head on my paws too, frustrated. But I just couldn't give up! I lifted my head and said, "You know, King, I know you think you're too old be useful to anyone, but let me tell you something-"

But I didn't get to say anymore. George came back. "Okay, gang, let's get ready for the show. What do you guys say?"

As the old saying goes, the crowd went wild. But this time, instead of barking my head off, I turned and looked at King. I guess I was pleading with my eyes, but all he would do was shake his head.

George went to King's cage and let him out, but King walked slowly with his head down.

"What's the matter, King?" George said. "I know you're famous for being a wandering fellow, but I bet we could find you a home today. So, you wanna be on the show?"

King didn't even bark, just wandered back into his cage and slumped down on the floor. He smiled at me, but all I saw was sadness in his big brown eyes. I couldn't bear it; I turned my head in George's direction.

George could read a dog's mind, too. He saw me looking at him and said, "Looks like you two have some talking to do." Then he opened my cage. I went over and plopped myself right next to King.

As soon as George left the room, I said, "Thank you, King."

He lifted his head and looked at me, confused. "King, do you remember that first talk we had?" "Sure I do."

Well, that's what kept me strong. Strong enough not to freak out when they abandoned me."

"Really, Smallone?"

"Yes, really. And I love you for that. That's why I want to see you happy. And King? It doesn't matter if you're not a little puppy anymore-"

He turned his head away, but I jumped up and went over to his other side. This time, he *had* to listen. He still wouldn't meet me eyes as I continued. "King, I just know that if you go on the show, and act as happy as you can, there'll be someone out there who's looking for a dog as smart and fine as you are. You just have to think of things you're good at."

King dropped his head to his paws and sighed. "Smallone, I love you too.

But-"

"No buts, King!" I yelled.

He was startled at first, but then looked at me and grinned. And when I thought about it, it *was* kind of funny. Me, a two-pound Chihuahua puppy yelling at a full-grown German Shepherd. But hey, I've always spoken my mind. So I kept right on doing it.

"Okay, King, let's hear it . . . what can you do?"

He thought a moment, looking at Lady practicing in the corner. "Well, I don't know about dancing or singing. But . . . I'm supposed to be a guard dog, and I'm used to looking for trouble. I could watch a bank, or someone's home, and look real mean so no one will come in . . . that is, to rob the place."

"That's right!" I said, and reached out to cuff his shoulder with my paw.

"You're King from the West Side. Who's gonna mess with *you*?"

And then, I remembered. "Hey, King," I said. "You know this squirrel named Squeaky?"

"Squeaky? Yeah, I know her. She's a cool squirrel. I've played chase with her a few times."

"I love Squeaky, and she loves you, too."

He looked embarrassed, but said, "Really? Where did you see her?"

"When I got dumped in the woods." "That where they left you?" I nodded.

"Yeah. Tied to a tree."

His face turned mean, and he growled. But I knew he wasn't growling at me. He was just mad at Dad and the boys.

"I can't believe those people," he snarled. "What did we-or you- do to them for them to treat us so bad?"

"I don't know, King, but it was Squeaky that gave me hope. She told me to look for you. That's what I was doing when I ran into Tom. He's the security man here."

King stiffened. "A guard?" From the way he acted, I thought he wasn't too fond of guards. Maybe, in the past, he'd had a bad experience with one.

"Yes, a guard," I said. "That's Tom. He's great. He brought me here."

King looked around. "Yeah, that was nice of him. It's a little confining, but better than being outside, I guess-especially for a little dog like you."

"That's my point, King," I said. "There *are* some nice people out there. Even people in uniforms have been nice to me. And Tom's the one who named me Smallone. Columbia is nice too-that's Tom's wife-but she gets sick when I'm near her. So they couldn't keep me at their house."

"Sorry to hear that, Smallone."

"Okay, enough about me. What are you going to do for the show?"

He sighed. "I keep telling you, I don't know. What can an old dog like me do?"

You know, when a German Shepherd sighs, it's really sad-looking. But his next words made *me* sadder: "Smallone, I know you're trying to help, but-"

"King, there's room for everyone here," I told him. "There are people out there who want you. We just have to let them know we're here, and that we want to be loved and give it back. That's all-"

Tom came through the door just then. "Okay, let's break a leg for me, guys. Hey, Smallone, you guys look great. I won't be surprised if you're all gone in a week. There are people out there who need all kinds of dogs.

Watchdogs, home dogs, or just to have as companions. People love you guys, so good luck, and I love all of you."

Finally, I could see some hope in King's eyes, and it was love I felt. Love for life, and love for one another. That's what counts.

After a while, George came in. "Guys, the network is here." The barking and meowing began. Gail and Terry came in and said, "Guys, quiet. Everyone quiet."

Everyone managed to calm down. Even the birds landed by their cage and went right in. But we were nervous, just sitting there waiting for the next thing to happen.

In came Lisa. "Good morning, everyone. Today's the day, are we getting ready? There's a lot of excitement out there. So let's have fun. Smallone, are you ready?"

When she said that, all of us dogs started to bark; the cats were meowing; the birds were flapping their wings and whistling.

"Guys, guys, no, not now," Lisa said. "They'll let us know when. George, could you quiet them down?"

"Lisa, they just want to show you they're ready," George said.

Lisa smiled. "I can see that for sure. Okay, I'll bring them in."

The door opened, and in came Johnny and Victor. "Hello, everyone," Johnny said. "They're here. Good morning, guys."

It wasn't five minutes before the door opened and in came five women, carrying all kinds of equipment. Gail said to the camera crew, "Whatever you need, ask Johnny, Victor and George."

One of the women holding a camera said, "Thank you for your help, guys."

Terry said, "This is Connie. She's in charge of the layout, and she has Bonnie and Angie that work with her."

Dr. Casey came in. "Hey, guys, you look good, are you ready? Okay, I wish all of you good luck and I hope this works out for you. I'll see you after the show. Break a leg for me."

"Ruff, Ruff!" I told him, and put my paws up.

He smiled at me. "Okay, Smallone, good luck." Then, to Connie, "Connie, if they're not ready now, they'll never be ready. They've been practicing for the last two weeks. Thanks a million."

Connie looked around. "Bonnie could you put that chair over here? Let's make it look a little more inviting. And is your section ready?" Bonnie nodded.

"Angie, how about your section?"

Angie laughed. "If I'm not ready now, I'll never be." Angie looked at all of us. "Connie, the dogs and cats look great. The birds, too. I sense there's something special about today." And then she saw the little puppy and me.

"Oh, my, there's a little Chihuahua and a Golden Lab. Aren't they beautiful?" As Angie said that, I couldn't help but notice the sadness in King's eyes. But when I winked at him, he gave me a smile. "Stay with the routine, and you'll be fine," I barked at him. Well, actually, it was a couple of yips. Gail had said to be quiet, and I was trying to obey.

Connie was behind the camera now. "Okay, in two minutes, I'm going to start rolling, so everyone get ready."

Gail and Terry got in front of the camera, and Connie called out, "Ready for the introduction . . . Okay, rolling."

"Hello, everyone," Gail said to the camera. "I'm Gail, and this is Terry.

Today, we have such beautiful pets for adoption from the Humane Society of Connecticut. These pets are bright, smart, clean and healthy. And most of all, they're loving. We also have two birds that sing. Listen! You can hear them as we speak. All these pets are in a need of a loving home."

Another camera panned to Minsk and Beauty. Gail said, "We also have two cats that are adorable. And look, they're doing a little dance. Look how pretty they look. They've all had their shots. Although they're not related, taking one doesn't mean you have to take the other. But they're a beautiful pair. They're very clean. The people that adopt these beautiful cats will be grateful to the Humane Society for their loving cats."

She waved toward King. "Up next, we have this beautiful new arrival, a German Shepherd. This dog is up there in experience. It's a loving dog and he loves kids. This dog takes charge wherever he goes, or wherever you want him to be. If you're in the market for a companion or a watchdog, this shepherd is for you."

The whole time Gail described him, I kept nodding at King. And he really did try hard to smile. I was so proud of him for trying. "Over here," Gail said, and pointed to the puppy, "we have a mixed Lab. A beautiful face, strong. And very smart."

At this point, Gail and Terry were just talking. We weren't dancing or anything! This wasn't good!

And suddenly, the camera turned to me.

"Here we have a Chihuahua," Gail said. "A very cute and smart dog."

I couldn't help it. I put my paws up and said, "Ruff! Ruff! Ruff!"

"What's that, Smallone?" Terry said, and smiled. "Gail, I think she wants you to open all the cages. Dr. Casey, if I open-"

At that moment, we couldn't wait any longer. We started barking, meowing, and whistling.

Dr. Casey laughed. "Okay, open all the cages. Gail, open King, Blackie and Lady's cages. George, how about playing a little music?"

The camera turned to him, and Dr. Casey said, "Gail, Lady and Blackie are going to dance. King is going to trot. Oh, my, look how nice they look!"

They all did look nice, just like Dr. Casey said. But then I heard Lady say, "Oh, no, Blackie, you stepped on my paw!" Blackie told her, "Don't worry about it, Lady. Not now! We're on camera!"

The birds were flying, and King started to jump as Prince trotted and turned. I started to leap just as high as I could. Terry and Gail saw me.

"Wow, she can jump!" Gail said.

"Okay, everybody, we have about three minutes left," Connie said.

"Gail, get the puppy," Terry said.

Gail ran fast, came back in a second, and placed the Lab right next to me.

# ROCKET & THE CONSTRUCTION WORKER

"Here, we have a little Golden Lab," Gail said. "This one doesn't know much of anything, because she's only six weeks old. This Lab will be great for kids."

Then Gail looked at the camera. "We'd all like to thank you for watching, and we all hope to hear from you soon. Right guys?"

We all gave her a round of barks, meows and whistles, then she turned back to the camera. "Thank you for your time from the Humane Society.

Take care, and take a pet. Thank you." "Cut!" Connie said.

The birds were flying crazy and whistling; the cats were hopping around, even singing. But King didn't look too happy. I asked him how he was feeling.

"Nice show we put on," King said. "Nice show everyone but *me* put on. Most of the time, I was just sitting there."

"King, don't worry," I said. "You were great. And you know what I think? Right now, there's someone who saw you, and they're wishing they had you in their house."

King turned his head away from me and toward the puppy, whom Gail had put back into the cage. "Look over there, Smallone. The puppy? She'll be fine. She'll find a home. But me? I don't think so."

I started to reply, but when I saw Lady and Blackie heading over, with their faces like thunderclouds, I knew something bad had happened.

"You almost made me trip," Lady said to Blackie.

"I did not, Lady," Blackie replied. "You have to keep up."

"Easy guys," I said. "You both were great! Now, what's wrong?"

George and Dr. Casey walked up then. "You guys did really well," Dr. Casey said, then chuckled. "After that show you put on, I hope I still have a job next week."

Tom came in and walked over to us. "Columbia just called and said the show was so beautiful, she cried. From happiness, of course." He turned to me. "Everyone is going to want you, Smallone. I have to pick you up tomorrow. Columbia wants to see you for a few minutes. That is, if you're still here."

"Ruff! Ruff! Ruff!"

"Easy, girl," he said, laughing. "We know you have it all. Hey that's not a bad name I gave you, is it?"

I wanted to tell him that the name was fine, and that I love him and Columbia, and that I'd never forget them for taking care of me at their home, and that they gave me love and strength. But all I could do was bark.

I think Tom understood, though; he turned and walked away with a tear in his eye.

I didn't remember to ask Lady and Blackie what they were arguing about.

We were all played out, so it wasn't long before the others fell asleep. But I couldn't sleep, because I couldn't help noticing King. He was sitting up, looking out of the window. When I heard a noise that sounded like he was crying, I called out to him. He turned around with those big brown eyes full of tears.

"What's wrong?" I asked.

"I don't care what you say, or anyone else says. I'll never be adopted, because I'm too old." He looked back at the window. "I'd be better off out there. At least I could see the whole sky out there."

"That's not so," I said.

"It *is* so. I keep telling you, nobody wants an old dog."

I sighed. "Okay, King, you're old. In fact, you're the oldest one here. But you know something, King? Someone's gonna call about that old German Shepherd, cause you're just the one they've been looking for-a kind and good-looking dog that takes charge and protects, and most of all, can be a friend."

He didn't speak for the longest time. Didn't look at me either. But finally, he turned his head back to me. "Is that what you see in me?"

"Yes, King, that's what I see. You're also a good leader, and you're liked and respected. That includes me, too. I'll always be grateful to you."

"For what, Smallone?"

"For giving me strength and courage when I needed it most." King looked at me and winked.

"I mean, think about it. You're the reason I ended up here in this nice place . . . „cause I was looking for you when I ran into Tom. You let me know I wasn't alone in feeling the way I did."

"Smallone?" His voice was so soft, I almost didn't hear him.

"Yes, King?"

"Did they treat you really bad? At the House of Misery?"

"Yeah. But now I'm glad they left me in the woods. If they hadn't, I would never have made it here."

I heard Lady and Blackie talking. Actually, they were arguing. And then I remembered what I forgot earlier.

Lady said, "Well, I know I tripped, because you stepped on my paw,

Blackie."

"You couldn't even notice it," Blackie replied. "I didn't make you trip."

"You did too, Blackie. And I-"

"Look, I saw what happened," I said, startling them. "And Lady, I know it upset you, but I really don't think Blackie meant it. Can you forgive him?

Please? For me?"

Lady sighed. "Oh, all right."

"Okay, so it's over," I said. "Thank you, Blackie, and Lady. Love you guys."

"We love you too," Lady called back.

"Sorry if we were annoying you," Blackie added.

"It's okay," I told them. Then I turned back to King. "King, I think we're going to be friends for a long time."

"I hope so, Smallone. He looked at the window again. "Well, it's late, and I'm sure you're tired. Let's get some sleep."

I heard keys, and it sounded like George, the way he makes them jingle as he walks. Sunlight was beginning to come through the window, and a new day was about to begin.

I looked around, and everyone else was moving too. And I heard the sounds of the other staff coming in.

I licked George's hand, and he said, "Well, Smallone, no one's called yet. But we just opened the office. So pretty soon, you might hear the phone ringing a lot."

The next thing I knew, Dr. Casey was coming in and saying good morning to everyone. Gail and Terry were next to arrive. Victor came in and went straight for King to check on him, then over to Blackie's cage to clean it up. As he worked, he talked to us.

"Guess what? My aunt Millie saw the show, and she wants to adopt the two birds! She'll be here at ten this morning."

When Victor said that, everyone started to bark, meow, and fly and sing with a whistle. Even King looked happy.

Dr. Casey came my way. He said, "Smallone, where's the little Golden Lab?"

I moved over and he said, "Oh, there you are. You're so small, I thought you'd disappeared."

Through the open door, I could hear the phones start to ring. Gail and Terry talked for a while, and then Gail came into the room. "Hey, guys, a lady by the name of Eileen called. She has an interest in the little Golden Lab."

Exciting news! As I looked at the others, I could see the happiness in their eyes, but sadness too. Happy that the show was a success, and that people were starting to call. Yet there was sadness because we all weren't going yet.

I felt the same way, I couldn't figure it out. The birds are going. My little friend is going. I shouldn't be sad, but happy. But, I think the best way to stop being sad is to make someone else happy. Or at least try to. "Guys, don't look so sad," I told the others. "We've only been open a little while, and we've already had two adoptions. Let's give it a chance. Let's feel good about the birds and the Lab." "Smallone, you're right," Lady said. "Let's give it some time." "So we agree to be happy for the next guy?"

When I said that, the barking, meowing, singing began.

Dr. Casey came in with Gail, and he was holding a camera. "Morning, guys. I brought my camera in so we could remember

# ROCKET & THE CONSTRUCTION WORKER

this day. How great you all were yesterday. So what ya say?" We said yes!

George, Victor and Johnny started to open the cages. Victor touched Prince on the head and asked, "Are you all right? You're kind of quiet."

Gail walked over. "He's probably just feeling cramped. It's a shame we have to keep these big dogs in cages so much. He'll be all right."

They gathered us together for the picture. The phone rang. When Gail came back, Dr. Casey asked, "So who was that?" "Oh, that's someone who has an interest in the shepherd. A Mr.

Gepeto. He'll be here around 11:30, he told me. He owns Gepeto's Auto Parts in Hunts Point."

Dr. Casey frowned. "In the Bronx? Did you tell him our policy? About not allowing anyone outside Connecticut to adopt? Well, usually."

Gail nodded. "He said „No problem. I'm just sure you'll make an exception. They'll love it there.'"

Dr. Casey thought a moment, then said, "When he gets here, we'll have Lisa interview him, just to be sure."

As Gail and Dr. Casey talked, I could see King's curiosity. His eyes opened and his ears stood straight up. He looked at me and smiled. I winked back at him.

As Gail readied to take our picture, I could see the doc looking at Prince. He turned to Terry and said, "He'll be all right. Gail's right. He just got a little cramped in the cage. With a little luck, he won't have to stay in it much longer."

I was glad to hear that, and so was Prince. The birds were flying upside down and whistling.

We were standing next to the sign that reads, "All Animals are Welcome at the Humane Society." "Come, everyone," Dr. Casey said. Victor said, "What about Prince?"

"Just bring Prince over here, he'll be all right here."

And guess what happened next? George picked me up and plunked me down right in the middle of the group, right before Dr. Casey snapped the picture!

## CHAPTER 6

# The Adoption

The phone rang again, and Lisa called out, "I'll get it!" We listened to her say, "Which one? The black dog, you mean? The black Lab?"

As she was saying that, we all looked at Lisa. She, in turn, was looking at Blackie. "Three o'clock tomorrow? . . . I must remind you that our policy is first come, first served. We don't hold pets. So try and make it as soon as possible. . . . That'll be fine. Thank you."

Lisa hung up the phone. The doc asked, "Who was that?"

"A lady by the name of Helen," Lisa replied. "She's in love with the black Lab. She knew a black dog just like the one we have. It used to live across the street from her. The house burned down, and the people moved away. Dr. Casey, she sounds like she really wants her."

Blackie's eyes opened wide, and her ears pointed straight up. She was so happy she started to bark. George, Johnny and Victor went back to cleaning up, and the girls went back to answer the phones.

The day passed fast. Just as the sun began to lower in the window, I heard a lady call out, "Victor, are you still open?"

Victor looked at Gail, and she gave the OK sign. Then he went to open the door.

"Victor," said Aunt Millie, "do you still have the birds?"

Victor kissed his aunt and introduced her to Gail. "Gail's in charge of the adoption."

Gail nodded and smiled at the elderly woman. "Millie, I hear you have an interest in our birds. We have two of them, and they're sisters."

"Sisters?" Aunt Millie said. "Would it be a problem if I took both of them?"

Gail hesitated, then said, "Let me get Lisa. She'll do the interview. Lisa?" "Yes, Gail."

"Could you interview Victor's Aunt Millie? She wants to adopt the two birds."

Lisa stuck her head into the room. "Millie, Victor told me so much about you . . . how you love birds and all."

"Oh, yes, Lisa, I love all God's creatures," Aunt Millie said. "But I live in a little apartment, so birds are the best pets for me, I think."

Victor got the birds from their cages and brought them to the desk. Aunt Millie went right up to the birds and whistled at them, and they whistled back. *She talks to birds,* I thought. *That's cool!*

A little while later, I heard Victor ask, "Lisa, how did it go?" "The interview went fine," Lisa said. "I was a little concerned about two birds, but Aunt Millie told me that her last pets were two birds. And she seems to know a lot about their care, so I think she'll do just fine. She just has to sign a few things. Then she can take them home. Maybe you could help her get them into her car?" "Oh, sure," Victor said.

I watched them help Aunt Millie load the birds into the car.

Through the open window, I heard Victor ask Lisa, "Thanks for staying late like this."

"Anytime, Victor. And it was nice to meet your aunt."

Aunt Millie spoke up, "Lisa, I have Victor over for dinner every Friday. I'd love it if you could join us this week."

Lisa smiled. "I'd love to, but only if Victor approves. He sees me more than enough around the Humane Society."

Victor laughed. "Oh, I don't mind at all. And hey, maybe we could take in a movie sometime?"

Lisa looked a little startled, but smiled and said, "Sure. That would be nice."

By the time Victor locked up, it was almost dark.

I heard Victor out in the hallway, then he said, "Oh, Dr. C, you're still here?"

"Not for long. I was just checking on Prince. See you tomorrow, Victor."

"Sure, Doc. Goodnight. Thanks for everything. And oh, how's Prince doing?"

"He seems a lot better now. Maybe all the excitement of the show. He'll be fine by tomorrow."

"Yeah. Maybe. Goodnight, Doc."

Victor came in to check on us one last time. "Smallone, it's been one day, and already we have the birds a home. King's going, Blackie, and the Golden Lab might be going. And oh, a lady by the name of Rita wants one of the cats. She'll be here tomorrow at 4:30."

I waited a moment, but . . . he didn't say anything about me!

I'm telling you, humans must be able to read minds! "Don't worry, Smallone," he said. "I know you're going to find a nice home, and a person that's going to love you and take good care of you. So keep the faith. Good things happen when you work at them . . . and you guys worked hard today." *Ring, Ring, Ring.*

Victor raced for the phone. "Hello, Humane Society, may I help you. . . . We sure do. . . . What's your name, sir? Hello, Mr. Jimmy Star. 12 noon? That'll be fine, Mr. Star. I'll leave a message for the staff you'll want to talk to. And oh, where do you live, Mr. Star? Maopac, New York? Oh. I'm sorry, Mr. Star, but we only allow residents of Connecticut to adopt. . . . I know you want the dog, but . . . why don't you come in for an interview anyway? The final decision isn't mine, you see."

Victor hung up the phone and came back to me. "Gee, we sure are getting lot of interest from New York. Smallone, someone has an interest in you. His name is Jimmy. Jimmy Star. He lives really near that guy in the Bronx. He said he'll be here around noon tomorrow." Victor smiled. "You see, Smallone? I told you someone was thinking of you. Now let me get out of here. It's almost six already.

As Victor put me in my cage, I couldn't help thinking of the phone call. So someone has an interest in me. And his name is Jimmy. Well, if he's like Billy or Nick or Dad, I don't want him. I don't want to go back to the House of Misery. Ever!

But Lisa will interview him. And judging from her interview of Aunt Millie, she's pretty picky.

I look at the others. King's probably going with that Mr. Gepeto. The birds are gone. My little roommate might be going too- to a lady with two sons. That will be good for little Goldie. And it's just been two days since we put on the show. It's looking good. And who knows? Maybe Mr. Jimmy Star will be a star in *Lisa's* book, too.

I could see Lady, not looking too happy. "Is there anything wrong?"

Blackie jumped in. "She just sure we're not going to be adopted, because of my stepping on her foot. Smallone, please tell Lady that isn't so!"

"Lady, the show went great. Don't worry about that. And you're looking great, as usual."

"Yes, but King is going, and the birds are gone. Blackie's going." She glared at Blackie. "Even your little friend's going. And Beauty and Minsk are going tomorrow. That leaves Prince and me. I just know it's because of Blackie. He made me trip when we were dancing."

"For once and for all, I didn't make you trip, Lady!" Blackie yelled.

Lady turned to him. "Yes, you did, Blackie!"

"Stop it, stop it!" I yelled at both of them. Then to Lady, "Let's give it some time, Lady, please? And Blackie, Lady loves you." Blackie nodded. "I know, Smallone. She's just worried."

"And you're still here too," Lady said to me. "What about you? Doesn't anyone have an interest in you yet?"

"Well . . . Victor just got off of the phone with a man that has an interest in me."

"Then why don't you look happy?"

"I . . . I don't know. Maybe because his name is Jimmy. It sounds like Billy."

"Oh, like your old owner, right?" "Yeah."

She gave me an understanding nod. "You know, Smallone, a lot of names sound alike. Haven't you noticed that about humans? They're all common sounds, like Blackie, Mackie, Cackie. Check him out, and then you could make that call."

"Huh? What call, Lady?"

"What I mean is, after you meet him, then you can decide if you want to go with him."

"I don't think he'll have much choice," Blackie said. Lady glared at him. "I didn't ask you anything, Blackie."

"Well, I heard my name. Why? Did you want to say you're sorry for carrying on about me stepping on your paw?"

"Well, you *did* step on my paw, and I'm probably not going to be adopted because of it."

I sighed and put my paws on top of my head. "Will you two stop it already? Please, Blackie. No one was talking to you anyway. She was just rhyming some names to make a point."

"Smallone?" Lady said. "Who knows? Mr. Jimmy Star might be the best thing that could happen to you."

That made me smile. "I like the way you think, my pretty friend. Thank you."

"No, Smallone. Thank *you* for everything. You brought a spark here, and good things are happening. You gave us all hope for a better tomorrow." "Thanks, Lady. Now, let's all try and sleep on it. It's been a long day."

Finally, Lady and Blackie agreed on something, and we all went to sleep.

Okay, I'll admit it. I stayed awake for a long time, and I couldn't help but to cry. Hey, even Chihuahuas cry sometimes. But not because I was sad, or even worried about tomorrow. I cried because I was happy that I met some good friends here. Sure, when we leave here, I probably won't ever see them again. But they would be in my heart forever.

I woke up to Lady's voice. "Smallone, it's so exciting! She's asking about Minsk and Beauty!"

We watched as Gail talked to a woman, then called out, "Lisa, could you being the two cats out here for Miss Poulas?"

Thankfully, Lisa left the door open in her hurry.

"Miss Poulas, I'm glad you like them," Lisa said after a while. "So let's do the interview next."

Dr. Casey came in and went right over to Prince, touched his head, looked at his mouth, ears. . . . He looked him over pretty good. "Prince, are you feeling better?"

"Ruff! Ruff!"

Then the doc said, "I'm sure you are, Prince," and laughed.

As Dr. Casey started to make his rounds, I could see Lisa coming from the office. Miss Poulas was right behind her, looking upset.

"I truly *am* sorry, Miss Poulas," Lisa said to her. "But you don't meet the income requirements for supporting two cats, and I really feel like they'll be too much for you."

"But I don't understand!" Miss Poulas said. "I love these cats and I'll take good care of them."

Well, Miss Poulas, we have guidelines we go by. And it costs more to care for a pet than most people think. I'm sorry." "How about one cat?" Gail said.

Lisa nodded. "She meets the requirements for one cat."

Gail turned to Miss Poulas. "Miss Poulas, how does one cat sound?" Miss Poulas nodded. "One cat sounds good. And I have an idea.

My friend wanted one of them, but I told her I wanted both of them. I'll tell her that all you could give me was one. She'll be here first thing in the morning. And she'll love the idea of getting the cat."

I could see Miss Poulas walking away with Beauty meowing, as Lisa took Minsk her back to her cage, meowing.

Things were still looking good. I mean, they didn't go to one home, but they could still see each other sometimes.

Things are moving on now. The door opened, and in came this big man. Boy, was he big! He went right over to Gail and said, "Hi, I'm Mr. Gepeto. I came for my beautiful dog, the big German Shepherd. And if it's all right with you, I would also like to adopt the mixed breed who was on the show-you know the yellow dog with the long hair."

Gail looked surprised. "Excuse me, Mr. Gepeto. You'd like *two* dogs?"

He nodded. "I have a big place, and they would be fine, and have each other to play with."

*Wow, that would be great for King and Prince!* I thought, and held my breath.

Gail said, "I think that'll work, Mr. Gepeto. But we'll have to wait until after the interview to decide."

"Of course, of course," Mr. Gepeto replied. "The show was great. Where's that little Chihuahua?"

"Oh, someone has an interest in her, and he'll be here around noon."

# ROCKET & THE CONSTRUCTION WORKER

"Oh, that's all right. I just wanted to see her." Gail pointed. "She's right over there."

I could see this big man coming my way. As he came over to the cage, the Lab barked at him. I'm sure he was scared. Hey, I was a little nervous myself! But he was nice to us.

Lisa said, "Mr. Gepeto, we have the dogs for you to get acquainted with in the yard. And after you do, Lisa will interview you."

When King came back in, King was crying.

"What's wrong, King?" I asked him. "Why are you crying?"
"Oh, Smallone," he said, "I just don't want to leave you here alone!"
"Look at it this way," I said. "You've been on the street all your life. Now you're getting up there, and it might not be so easy for you anymore. And look how beautiful things are going for you. You're going to have a home, and Prince is going with you. And you'll have a master that loves the both of you. You're going to be happy, King."

"But . . . what about you? It's almost noon, and he isn't here yet. That Jimmy fellow. What if he never shows up?"

I hadn't thought about that. "Yeah. Yeah, King, you're right." "Maybe he had car problems," Prince said. "Humans are always talking about that." I nodded. "Maybe." *Or maybe he's changed his mind.*

But I couldn't let my worries spoil their happiness. "Anyway," I said, "I'll always think of this as the happiest time of my life."

We were just finishing saying our goodbyes when the door opened. Gail entered, then Lisa, and then big old Mr. Gepeto.

"Good news, guys," Lisa said. "Mr. Gepeto qualifies for two dogs."

Mr. Gepeto walked to King and Prince's cage and called out, "Over here, over here."

King walked to Mr. Gepeto's side of the cage and began licking his hand. Then Prince came up and did the same.

As Mr. Gepeto led them from the cage area, he looked back and saw Minsk, Blackie, Lady, and all the rest of us. They all looked happy, and sad-a look I was getting used to. I barked, "Ruff!

Ruff! Ruff!" And all the other dogs joined in. Except Minsk, who meowed, "Goodbye! Good luck!"

And then this man came into the room, and went right over to Gail. "I'm sorry I'm late," he said, "but I hit traffic, a lot of traffic. Please tell me you still have her!"

"Who would that be, sir?" "The Chihuahua."

"Oh, well . . . I'm sorry." But I could see Gail smiling at Terry. "Don't tell me you don't have her!" the man said. "My radiator overheated three times.

The car is still smoking.

"Oh, I'm only kidding," Gail said. "Sorry about that."

The man started to laugh. "Whew! I thought I'd lost out on a great pet!"

The next thing I knew, Terry was picking me up and taking me to the front desk.

"Mr. Star, would you like to get acquainted with Smallone in the yard?" Gail said.

"Yeah, sure. I'd like that."

And we all headed outside. As Terry put me down, I went to the bathroom right away. I could hear Terry telling Mr. Star that was a good sign. Why, I don't know. But hey, if Terry said it was a good sign, I'd go along with it.

"I'll be back in a few minutes," Terry told Mr. Star. "Okay, Terry, thanks."

As soon as she left, he knelt down and held out his hand. "Hey, little guy.

You want to come home with me? I saw you on TV, and you look great."

I didn't go to him right away. Instead, I just looked at him. Was he going to be *another* human who thought I was a boy?

But, he seemed nice enough. He was dressed in jeans, a T-shirt, and tan boots. He was tall, as tall as Tom, and had dark hair and a mustache. His eyes were as green as Minsk and Beauty's. He reached out and held me up, way up above his head. "Smallone you are," he said, "but I think I could do better than that for a name. How about Rocky? Oops, you're a girl. Sorry about calling you a guy earlier."

I gave a little bark to let him know that was all right . . . that I was used to it. But he must have thought I was barking because I was scared of being held up so high. He pulled me back down into his arms and said, "Well, since you're a girl-dog, „Rocky' won't do. How about Rocket?"

*Humm, not bad,* I thought. *Got a nice ring to it. And hey, since we might be living together pretty soon, I think Mr. Star's too formal. How about Jimmy instead?*

And I swear, *he* read my mind too! "Rocket it is," he said. "Let's go, Rocket, and see if they'll let me have you."

The longer I thought about it, the better I liked the idea. I mean, even though he thought I was a guy at first, and held me up maybe a little higher than I liked, Mr. Jimmy Star definitely had a way with names!

As we walked to the front of the desk where Gail was sitting now, Gail saw us. "So how did it go?" "I want her," Jimmy said.

"Okay, Mr. Star. Lisa will interview you in a minute." "Excuse me? I'm not looking for a job. Interview for what?" "Oh, to see if you meet the guidelines, Mr. Star."

"Okay, girls, whatever," he said. And that was the same thing I would have said too!

I went back to my cage, and a little while went by. Then I overheard Gail ask Lisa, "How did it go?"

"No problem, Gail. Everything's okay. Mr. Star lives outside the state, but everything else looks good, so I've decided to make an exception."

Gail asked him, "Did you give her a name?" "Yes, I did. Her name is Rocket."

"What a neat name!" Terry said.

Mr. Star smiled. "Thank you for thinking so, Terry."

Gail patted my head. "Take good care of yourself. And, Smallone . . . I mean, Rocket, we'll always remember you. For what you did here for the others. You'll be missed."

I heard Mr. Star ask, "Gail, what did she do? Did my Rocket do something great?"

"She sure did," Gail said. "That was the best adoption show we ever had. You should have seen her, always cheerful, always encouraging the other animals to do their best. I really think her behavior had something to do with it."

Mr. Star smiled. "I knew she was a winner. Thank you for holding her for me."

Lisa laughed. "Rocket will always be a winner here, and Gail's right-we'll never forget her."

"Ruff! Ruff!" Back at you, girls!

## CHAPTER 7

## Jimmy And Rocket Go Home

Jimmy took me to his car, he sat me in the front seat, and as I looked at him, he smiled at me. It was already looking up!

As he smiled at me, I couldn't help but feel good inside. "Hey, Rocket," he said, "I think the car's cooled down. These old Eldorados recover fast."

I didn't know what "Eldorado" meant, but the car was big and brown. That's all I could make out before he sat me down, started the car and said, "Excuse me Rocket, would you like a little air?" He reached over and rolled my window partway down. "Will that do?" he asked. And then he kissed me on the head!

I'm telling you, at that moment, I felt great. I couldn't wait to get home . . . wherever that was. As long as I was with Mr. Jimmy Star, anywhere was just fine with me!

Before I knew it, we pulled into this driveway that went up a big hill. Jimmy shut the car off and said, "Rocket, we're home."

Oh, this was a big house! And opposite the house, there was a lake. Lots of places to explore!

Jimmy opened my door and I hopped out, and we started playing right there. He was jumping around with me, and every time he said, "Come on, Rocket, jump up, up!" I jumped a little. I think he was just as happy to be with me as I was to be with him!

After a few minutes, he picked me up, and we went through this side door into a big room. There was a bathroom and kitchen off the room, and a really big bed in the middle of the room. And right next to the big bed was a little bed. My size!

Jimmy said, "Up! Up!" I hopped up, and he looked at me with a happy expression on his face.

We weren't in the house five minutes before the phone rang.

"Hello," he said, and listened a moment. "Yes, I do. . . . She's a little dog. . . . Yes, I'll pick up after her, Mrs. Lipsky. Have a good day. Bye." He hung up, then turned to me. "Hey, Rocket, we might have some problems with Mrs. Lipsky. But whatever happens, we'll be together. Love you."

"Ruff! Ruff!" (By now, I guess you know that means, "And I love you, too, Jimmy!")

Some time went by, and then he told me, "Well, Rocket, I have to get back to work. But I won't have to stay late. Later, we'll go in the yard and then walk by the lake and see the ducks. We'll bring some bread with us, okay?"

It wasn't too hard to wait until Jimmy came back; in his place, there were lots of things to explore and smell. As soon as he got home, he put a leash on me and we went down the long driveway and walked to the lake. At first, I thought I'd hate the leash, because of all the things that happened the last time I wore one. But it didn't bother me. In fact, I felt great. The birds were flying, the ducks were quacking, and there was a sense of peace in the air as we approached the lake. We saw the ducks dunking their little heads in the water and coming up with fish, and birds were flying low.

Jimmy started throwing bread into the water. And that's when I got scared—the birds were coming from all over to get the bread. Out of the water, out of the sky. Everywhere! And they were all quacking and flapping their wings, too, making a terrible amount of noise. There must have been at least a hundred of them.

# ROCKET & THE CONSTRUCTION WORKER

I barked at them and started to pull back. Jimmy noticed and said, "Okay,

Rocket, time to leave."

Did I mind? No way! Even Jimmy was looking a little nervous by then.

We walked back up the road, and the birds started to follow us! Jimmy looked down at me and said, "Let's run, Rocket, they're coming."

We left them in the dust and were home in a matter of minutes. Jimmy took my leash off and rubbed my head, smiling. "That was a close one, Rocket."

I agreed, but I was happy. I had fun running with him. It was a little scary, but nice. And I was so tired, I was yawning!

Jimmy made a nice little bed for me, with blankets, a pillow and some stuffed animals. One of them looked like King, but before I even had a chance to miss him, Jimmy said, "Hope King and Prince are doing well, don't you?"

"Ruff."

I looked at him getting into bed, and laid my head on the stuffed dog that looked like King. It was nice here. Nice and quiet . . .

Next thing I heard was the alarm clock going off. Jimmy got out of bed, put some clothes on and said, "Come on, Rocket, time to go out."

Man, was this great, or what? I got to go outside two days in a row!"

Jimmy put my leash on, and to the lake we went . . . this time, without bread.

We had a nice walk-the birds didn't bother us this time. As soon as we entered the house, the phone rang. Jimmy picked it up and said, "Hello? . . . What? . . ." He walked to the door and looked at a little box next to it. "I don't know. It's been on 55 since I got here. I never touched it . . . Okay . . . Bye, Mrs. Lipsky."

Seeing the look on Jimmy's face, I was reminded of the feeling I used to get around Dad—sick and scared at the same time. Somehow, I didn't think Mrs. Lipsky was a nice person. And it was obvious Jimmy wasn't happy. Maybe this was *his* House of Misery.

Jimmy hung up the phone, sighed, and looked down at me. "Rocket, I think this is going to become a problem sooner rather than later. So let's get ready, okay, cutie?"

Whatever he wanted, I was willing to do.

The next thing I heard was a phone ringing. He laid me down on my blanket, and I heard him say, "Hello? . . . Yes, everything's good, Mrs. Lipsky. . . . Yes, she has her shots. . . . What? You want me to keep her on a leash? You mean, inside the apartment? Ah, sure, Mrs. Lipsky. Bye-bye."

This time when he hung up the phone, he sounded mad. "Yeah, right! I'll keep you on a leash in your own home. She ever comes in here, you know what to do . . . scare her. But don't bite her. We don't want to hurt her." He thought a moment, then said, "She's becoming a problem. Rocket, we're not going to last long here. But as long as we're together, we'll be all right. I don't think she wants us here, anyway." He gave a bitter chuckle. "Maybe she didn't want *me* here, either. I'm going to start looking for someplace else for us."

*Scare her?* Did he really mean that? I've never scared anybody before. Not even Squeaky the squirrel, and I'm bigger than she is. But I love Jimmy for saying, *But as long as we're together, we'll be all right.* Because that's what I was looking for, too: someone to be with me through good times and bad times. To be loved, and to love someone the way I wanted to be loved.

"This isn't a good time for me," Jimmy was saying. "I just got separated from my wife, and I'm not making that much money. I've been out of construction jobs for about two months, and things are tight. But I love you, and you're with me. I have to pick up my son today." He gave me a big smile and rubbed my head. "JJ's going to love you, Rocket. Be nice to him. Don't bite him."

*Hey, Jimmy has a kid? It just gets better and better! And bite him? Are you kidding?* "Ruff!" I said.

Jimmy chuckled. "It sounds like you understand me, Rocket." Well, why not? Dogs are a lot smarter than humans think.

Jimmy left to pick up his son. I'd already investigated everything in the room I could reach. I even found some sliding glass doors, hiding behind some curtains. All of that running around tired me out. So I plopped down on my blanket, laid my head on the stuffed German Shepherd, and fell asleep.

I guess I must have been dozing. At one point, I heard someone walking down the steps in the back of the house where the garage was . . . and the door started to open!

I jumped up and started barking and barking and showing my teeth. The door opened a little more, and a little elderly woman opened the door real quick, came inside, and moved to the little box that was on the wall.

Hey, no one was allowed in this apartment except Jimmy and me. This was *our* place! And since Jimmy wasn't here, it was up to me to protect it. I ran toward her, kept on barking, and jumped really high-high enough to bite her arm. But just as I reached her, she stepped back outside and closed the door. My head banged into the door, and I fell.

It had been a little cold in the room when Jimmy left, but soon, it started getting really hot in there. I got so tired and dizzy, I laid down on the blanket again.

The next thing I heard was a key going into the door. It was Jimmy and a young boy.

"Man, it's really hot in here!" Jimmy said, then called to me.

"Rocket, Rocket, here girl!"

I was still dizzy from the heat, but I had to get to Jimmy. I ran to him, and he picked me up and introduced me to the boy. "JJ," he said, "meet Rocket.

And Rocket, meet my son, JJ."

JJ was maybe about Nick's age, fourteen or fifteen, with short blonde hair and lots of muscles. He was nice to me right away. He let me chase him, and then I let him chase me.

The phone rang.

"Dad, the phone," JJ said. "You want me to get it?" "Sure, JJ."

"Dad, it's some lady. She said her name is Mrs. Lipsky. Isn't that your landlady?"

Jimmy's face turned kind of mean. "Okay, JJ. Thanks. And hey, could you take Rocket out front a bit?"

"Sure, Dad. Come on, Rocket."

Twice in one day? I *love* this place!

JJ and I passed the old woman as we were going outside. But then he said, "Oh, I know . . . Dad has a ball. He bought it when he told me he was looking for a dog. Let's go get it."

Just as JJ opened the door, I heard Mrs. Lipsky say, "If you turn up that thermostat again, you'll have to leave!"

But I don't think JJ heard her. "Hi, Dad," he said. "Where's the ball?" "What's *that*?" Mrs. Lipsky said, looking at me.

"That's my dog, Rocket. I told you about her." Jimmy's face looked kind of mean.

Mrs. Lipsky glared at Jimmy. "*This* is the one you leave in the house?"

"Yes, it is, Mrs. Lipsky."

"Are you going to chain her up? Cause if there's an emergency, I need to come in your apartment."

"Sure I'll chain her up, Mrs. Lipsssky." "Excuse me, what did you say?"

"Mrs. Lipsky. That's what I said. No problem. But she's so small, she can't hurt anyone." He shook his head as if to say, *Chaining my dog in her own house? I don't think so!*

And then, I figured out why she'd come into the apartment when Jimmy was gone, and messed with that little box. I wanted to tell Jimmy that it was *her* who made it so hot in here. And I felt bad for him that Mrs. Lipsky was giving him a hard time. Now, I wish I *had* caught her arm when I jumped up at her. *No, maybe not*, I immediately thought. *Jimmy would only get into more trouble.*

# ROCKET & THE CONSTRUCTION WORKER

They talked a moment more, then Jimmy's face got all funny. "By the way, Mrs. Lipsky, how did you know the thermostat was on 80 degrees? You never looked at it when you came in, and you can't see it from where we're standing . . . unless you put it on 80 degrees yourself, maybe?"

"Never you mind, Jimmy," she said. "Just make sure it stays on 55 degrees."

When she left, I could see the sadness in Jimmy's eyes when he turned. He smiled to reassure me, but even his smile looked sad.

"Rocket, I think we're going to have problems here. We'd better start looking for a place." He glanced at his son. "I'm too far away for JJ, anyway."

"You have to move?" JJ said.

Jimmy nodded. "Yeah. But I think it'll be a good idea. She doesn't want me here, anyway. As soon as I come home the phone rings, and it's always her complaining about something or another. She's nuts. And I'm glad I'm going. I don't why she rented this apartment to me in the first place "

"Dad, where you going to move to?"

"I don't know. But I have to find a place where Rocket will be all right."

"Ruff! Ruff!" I wanted to tell him that wherever he goes, I wanted to go. That I love him because he always thinks of me. I could only bark, but I think he understood; he smiled at me. And this time, his smile wasn't so sad.

JJ played with me for a while. As we played, Jimmy made dinner. Soon we were all having dinner, and Jimmy and JJ were joking with each other. And I just knew everything would be all right. Not every landlord was like Mrs. Lipsky, and we would find another place. A *good* one. I just knew it!

The morning came so fast! It seemed like no time before I could hear the birds whistling and the ducks quacking at the lake. It was a lovely sound. But I still felt bad that Jimmy had to move cause of me. As I lay there on my blanket, I thought, *Maybe I'll leave, and then maybe he can stay if he tells his landlady that I left. Yeah, that's what I'll do when he takes me out-I'll run away. Then maybe he and his son can stay here.*

I felt bad thinking that, „cause I know they love me. But it's a nice place by the lake. They'll be happy here.

Next, I had to decide where to go when I ran away. I couldn't decide if I should head back to the Humane Society, or just take off on my own. But going back to the Humane Society might not work out. I don't even think I'm in Connecticut anymore. In fact, I'm not really sure where I am.

I thought and thought. I remembered Gail saying something to Jimmy about living in Mahopac. Yeah, that's right . . . Mahopac, that's where we live. Yeah, I remembered now. Mahopac. But didn't King and Prince go to Mr. Gepeto's auto parts yard, and it wasn't in Connecticut either? My head shot up. *Yeah, I'm close to King. Wait a minute! No, he went to Hunts Point. That's in the Bronx. I heard him tell Gail. And I don't know where the Bronx is, either.*

A little time went by, and JJ and his dad got up and got dressed.

I heard Jimmy call, "Hey, JJ, would you like some French toast?" "Sure, Dad."

"Why don't you take Rocket for a walk by the lake, and come back in about 15 minutes."

"Sure, Dad. Come on Rocket, let's put your leash on. Here girl, right over here, that's a girl."

"JJ, you think Rocket would like some?"

"I don't know Dad, why don't you ask her?" "French toast, Rocket!"

"Ruff! Ruff!"

Jimmy laughed, then said, "Don't let Rocket jump in the lake. She's a jumper."

# ROCKET & THE CONSTRUCTION WORKER

The ducks were making a lot of noise quacking, but the weather was nice. After about 15 minutes, I jumped into JJ's arms, and we headed back to the house.

As we were about to go into the apartment, Mrs. Lipsky came up the driveway. "JJ!" she called.

I turned around and showed my teeth, „cause I don't like her.

JJ kept on walking, ignoring her, and we made back to the apartment.

The phone rang just as Jimmy and JJ sat down to eat. The caller was . . . you guessed it . . . Mrs. Lipsky.

Jimmy talked to her for a minute, then turned around and said, "JJ, did you ignore my landlady?"

"I saw her, Dad," JJ whispered, "but I didn't speak to her."

With a sigh, Jimmy put the phone to his ear and apologized to her. Then he listened a moment, then said, "What? Don't worry, if I find a place, I'll be out by Friday."

In spite of Mrs. Lipsky's phone call, we had a nice breakfast. They were laughing and talking about hockey, football, baseball, all kinds of things. It's funny; even though they knew they had to move soon, they seemed to be having a ball.

Later, they started throwing the ball around. I was in the middle trying to catch it, and they talked about how high I could jump. Which was definitely true. While they played, Jimmy told JJ how he came to find me at the Humane Society of Connecticut. That's when I found out that my jumping was what impressed Jimmy the most.

After a while, Jimmy said, "So, do you have time to hang out or what?"

"Not really, Dad. Mike's going to pick me up around 4:30. I have to get ready."

I'd heard JJ mention the name before, and wondered who it was. I guess Mike is JJ's friend.

"Where are you and Mike going?" Jimmy asked.

"A birthday party." JJ paused, then added, "It's supposed to be outside, but I don't know. There were some big rain clouds outside earlier."

"Well, inside or out, I hope you have a good time."

"Dad, how did you make it up to Connecticut in your old car?" Jimmy laughed, then said, "I don't know how, but I did. But, boy, was she smoking. I had to pull over three times. That's what took me so long to get there. I'm glad they held Rocket for me. She's the best."

A while later, JJ said, "Okay, Dad, ready?"

"Yes, I am. I'll leave Rocket here, and I'll go over to the club after I drop you off."

JJ grinned at Jimmy. "You still go over there?" Jimmy nodded.

When they left, I changed my mind about running away. I mean, Jimmy didn't seem mad at me, just Mrs. Lipsky. So maybe he didn't mind moving. I'm going to stay with him till he doesn't want me anymore.

I could hear someone at the back door. Maybe it was the landlady! I ran to it, barking. I could hear the garage open and close. Yeah, it was her. I bet if I'd gone with Jimmy, she would've come right in. Maybe even done worse things this time.

I could see a car pulling down the driveway. She was leaving. Good!

After a while, I went to my blanket and laid my head down. That's when I saw a flash of light, then heard a big boom of thunder. I looked at the window; it was raining. I started to get cold, so I cuddled under my blanket to wait till Jimmy made it back home.

The rain stopped after a really long time, and it got dark. I could see the stars and the moonlight in the dark blue sky overshadowing the lake. It was beautiful. I wish we could stay here. But what good is staying when where you live makes you feel miserable? You have to feel good all around, in and out; otherwise, it doesn't work. You have to be happy. And as long as you're good, good things will happen to you. Maybe not right away, but they'll be coming your way soon.

I started to think of all my friends at the Humane Society. Wondered if that little cute Lab was adopted by that lady with the two boys. And Prince. And Minsk. Did that lady ever come for her? And all the others. I hoped they were all doing good, and in good hands. I guess when a pet gets adopted, anything can happen. But I'm lucky. I'm staying with Jimmy. I know he loves me, and I love him, and that's all I want in life . . . to be loved. Happiness comes from that.

Before I closed my eyes, I looked at the window. I could see the moonlight. It felt so nice and warm under my blanket. And it was nice knowing that I wasn't alone in this beautiful life of mine. Sure, it *wasn't* nice living with the boys and Dad. But now, I knew there were good people out there. It was all about timing, I think. Everybody needs someone, even us dogs. We need families that will love us and play with us. Take care of us. They need us like we need them. There were people who don't have anyone. But that's where the adoption comes in with the interviews. „Cause they really want to be careful who adopts us dogs. Life is tough enough, and we don't need people like the boys and their dad in the House of Misery.

I was trying to stay up and wait for Jimmy. I guess I didn't do a good job; I was out in no time.

I opened my eyes. The sun was blazing through the windows onto the floor. I turned to look at Jimmy's bed. He was sleeping like puppy, all curled up in his blanket. I didn't even hear him come in last night. That's how tired I was.

I got up and went over to the sliding doors. I could see the yard. Not only were there ducks, but also swans! I barked at them.

The next thing I heard was Jimmy saying, "Quiet, Rock, quiet please. I had a long night last night."

Up I went, hopped right onto Jimmy's bed and started kissing Jimmy all over the face.

"Stop it, stop it, cutie."

So I stopped, thinking he was mad at me.

Then he said, "Come here. Give me more kisses." He picked me up, shook me a little, then kissed me on the head and said, "Hey, Rocket, did you have a nice time yesterday with my boy?"

"Ruff! Ruff!"

"I'm glad you did. I went over to the club. Told a few friends about what happened. They said they didn't think it would be a problem moving by Friday. And if we don't find anything by Friday, we could stay at their friends' house for a few days. That was nice of them."

Like I said, there are a lot of good people in the world. And it looked like I was about to meet a bunch of them. If they were anything like Jimmy Star, I was set for life!

## CHAPTER 8

## Jimmy & Rocket Move

We went to the lake. Even with the big swans, it was nice. On the way back to the house, I heard meowing. I looked up and saw a cat in the bay window of another house, walking around really frantic. I pulled on the leash, and Jimmy turned to me and asked, "What's wrong, Rocket?"

I pulled the leash toward the house. Jimmy looked in the direction I was pulling. "Rock, we don't live there."

I pulled so hard, he let go of the leash, and I ran to the window. Well, guess what? It was Minsk!

I put my paws on the window, she did the same. Jimmy came over. "Hey, Rocket, you know the cat?" "Ruff! Ruff! Ruff!"

Jimmy stared at the cat through the window. "Yeah, it looks like one of the cats that was on the TV show with you." He chuckled.

"Hey, what you know . . . you met a friend here."

As Jimmy was talking, the door opened and a lady stepped out.

"Hello," she said. "You seem to be pretty excited about my cat. May I help you?"

"Well, my dog Rocket seems to know your cat."

The lady smiled. "Oh, she does, does she? Come here, Lou Lou!"

"Hey, wait a minute," I barked. "Her name is Minsk." But then, *my* name was different now, so maybe hers was too. And hey, Lou Lou is a pretty neat name.

Minsk and I had a reunion. She didn't exactly come up to me and hug my neck, but as soon as I quit barking, she reached out and stroked her paw on my nose.

"Oh, look at that," I heard the lady say. "They sure do know each other.

My name is Miss Lee. Do you live around here?"

"Yes," Jimmy said, "we do. But we're moving Friday."

"Oh, what a shame. First time I've seen your dog. Her name is . . . ?"

"Rocket."

"Rocket? How cute she is!"

"She seems to know your cat," Jimmy said. "How long have you had her?"

"Only a week."

"A week? Where did you get her from?" "The Humane Society."

"Of Connecticut, right?"

Miss Lee nodded. "Yes. How did you know?"

"That's where I adopted Rocket from. That's where they know each other. That's why she got so excited. They put on a great show together, didn't they? I remember hearing on the news . . . . I think this is the first time in their history that all the pets were adopted after they put on a show."

"Yes," Miss Lee said. "Sorry I missed it. My sister saw it."

"What's your sister's name?"

"Helen."

"Yes, she adopted a black dog from there," Jimmy said. "A dog named Blackie. I think she knew the dog from before. Something about a fire."

Of course, I didn't listen to what they said too closely. I was too busy catching up with Minsk . . . uh, I mean Lou Lou. Turns out, she's as happy with her new owner as I am with mine. See, I told you-happiness usually comes when you find the right situation!

As we were leaving, I barked to say goodbye, and told Lou Lou that we were leaving Friday. She looked sad and happy: happy for me that I have a good owner, but sad „cause I'll be leaving. I hoped Lou Lou's sister, Beauty, was good hands, too. Sisters and brothers grow up sometimes, and they move on, but they still love each other. In Beauty and Lou Lou's case, it was good to know that the love they had for each other was still there. For that, I was blessed.

We went back to the house, and Jimmy started taking pictures off the wall. He had some nice pictures, like a horse, and a picture of a big ship sinking next to an iceberg. The horse I recognized, but I didn't know what the iceberg picture was about. There were a lot of pictures with JJ. At one point, I could see a tear at the corner of his eye. So I walked over to him and rested my head on his boot. He leaned down, picked me up, kissed me on the head and said, "Don't worry, Rock, we're going to be all right. I have to see a friend of mine about an apartment tomorrow. Let's keep our fingers crossed and ask God for some help in this. If we leave it up to Him, the results can't come out any better. I'm going to do a few things, then we'll eat. Okay?" No problem there!

That night, we had dinner, and went for a walk down by the lake. We passed Minsk's . . . I mean, Lou Lou's house. I looked up at the house, but I didn't see her. Still, it felt great that she did good for herself. Maybe I'd see her tomorrow.

When we got back, Jimmy said, "I have to see a few friends, but I won't be long. Watch the fort for me." He grabbed his jacket and left. As he left, I saw sadness in his eyes. I started wondering about life in general. Not only we animals have it hard, but sometimes, humans do, too. But I loved Jimmy, and I knew he loved me too.

The next morning, I saw Jimmy sleeping on his bed. I guess I must have fallen asleep right after he left. Didn't even hear him come in.

After I gave him his good-morning licking and he stopped laughing, his face got serious. "Hey, Rocket, I have good news and bad news. What do you want first? The good news? I get it. Okay, here it is. We found a place. Now the bad news: We have to move tomorrow."

The bad news didn't sound so bad, but the good news was great. We found a place! Jimmy got off the bed. He made French toast again, with the special ingredient that made it taste so good.

A little later, he said, "Hey Rocket, what say we walk down by the lake one more time. And maybe we'll see Lou Lou, say goodbye."

He made a phone call, and he hung up the phone, he said, "Well, it looks like everything's all set. Let's go do our walk. It'll be the last time you and I have to deal with the ducks-or Mrs. Lipsky, either."

And that all sounded just fine to me!

We went to say goodbye to Miss Lee and Lou Lou. But we didn't see anyone there, and there was no car in the driveway. "Maybe she'll be back before we leave," Jimmy said.

I hoped so. I'd like to say goodbye to her. We walked down by the lake and said goodbye to all the ducks and birds. Jimmy wasn't saying too much. As we walked back to the house, I started to feel kind of sad. Not for me, but for Jimmy.

When we made it back inside, the phone rang.

"Hello? . . . What? . . . Yeah, today. We'll be out of here by 3 p.m. How about my security deposit? . . . Call me in a week? For what? . . . Oh, okay. Whatever."

He hung up the phone and said, "I have to deal with that *blank* one more time, and that's it. Oh, she gets me crazy!"

He started packing a few things, and I went to my blanket for a nap. The next thing I heard was Miss Lee talking to Jimmy. So I did, after all, get to say goodbye to Lou Lou!

"I want to thank you again, Rocket," Lou Lou said. "For what, Lou Lou?"

"For what you did for all of us at the Humane Society. I'll never forget you. You'll always be in my heart, and I love you."

"I love you too, Lou, Lou." We hugged each other, and I could hear Miss Lee calling, "Lou Lou, time to go, Lou Lou!" Lou Lou walked back to Miss Lee, and I could see tears in her eyes.

I guess I had teary eyes, too. Jimmy said, "What do we have here? Tears?" And he hugged me.

A little time went by, then I heard a noise coming up the driveway. Jimmy looked at the window and said, "Okay, Rocket, you're about to meet my friends."

And I got to meet Dean and Pete. Dean and Pete were friends, but didn't look much alike. Dean had blonde hair, and Pete had dark hair and a mustache like Jimmy's. They were both fast workers. Soon, Dean turned to Jimmy and said, "Is that everything?"

"Yep," Jimmy replied. "You came on strong. I owe you big-time." "What are friends for, Jimmy?" Pete said.

Looks like Jimmy had good friends too-just like me. Dean drove the truck, and Jimmy and I followed in his car. And we left that crazy landlady's house for good.

After a while, we came to this big house. Dean rang the front doorbell, and a man came to the door.

"Hi, Anthony," Dean said. "This is my friend Jimmy, and his pal, Rocket."

Anthony smiled at Jimmy, then me, and said, "Hi guys, come on in. Make yourself at home. Dean tells me you need a place."

"Yeah, just until I find an apartment," Jimmy said. "I really appreciate your offer."

"No problem. Any friend of Dean's is a friend of mine."

Jimmy looked at me. "Come on, Rocket. I'll make you up a nice bed. All I have to do is get adjusted, and I'll be right back to take you out."

Anthony reached out and patted my head. "How old is she?"

"She's a year old."

"She's so cute." Anthony smiled at me when he said it, and I had a good feeling.

"Thanks," Jimmy replied. "Oh, wait, I forgot to set up her nightlight. Be right back."

Anthony chuckled. "You bring her nightlight with you, too? Hey, Jimmy, you really take good care of that dog." Jimmy shrugged.

"Why not? She's the best." "Ruff! Ruff! Ruff!" (Hey, I'll second that!) Anthony looked at me. "Does she bark all night?"

Jimmy shook his head. "No. Just when she's happy." "Oh, that's cool."

Jimmy closed the door of our new room, and I headed for my blankets.

Maybe we were in a strange house, but I felt better about this one. Especially since I had someone who loved me and wanted to take care of me.

I could hear some talking through the door, but I was so tired, I think I could have slept through an elephant stampede by them. I lay down on my blanket and closed my eyes.

When I woke up, it was morning again, and I didn't know where I was . . . until I heard Jimmy talking to Anthony. He was thanking Anthony again for putting us up for the night. And boy, I had to go to the bathroom!

I raced to the door and scratched on it. "Ruff! Ruff! Ruff! Ruff!"

I heard Jimmy say, "Anthony, I better take Rocket out for a bit before she explodes."

# ROCKET & THE CONSTRUCTION WORKER

The door opened, Jimmy scooped me up, and we headed outside. Boy, I couldn't hold it anymore. I'm glad there were woods.

After we went back inside, the phone rang.

"It's for you," Anthony called out. "It's Dean."

"Hey, Dean, how you doing?" Jimmy said. "Yeah, we're all ready. Half an hour sounds good. Thanks again."

Dean drove up, said hello to Anthony, then said, "Well, we're heading over to Bobby's. With all that property, he must have something."

"Yeah, right," Anthony said. "Okay, Jimmy and Rocket. Take care, and I hope everything works out for you guys."

I know I'm moving around a lot, but at least I'm moving with someone, and I'm not alone. And it looks like Jimmy knows a lot of people, and they all want to help him. Kind of like all my friends at the Humane Society, don't you think?

Soon, we were at Bobby's place. And it was big! The biggest place I've ever seen.

"Hey, Dean, what's up?" Bobby said.

Dean introduced Jimmy and me, and Bobby said, "Hey, I know Jimmy. And who's that little cutie you have there?" Jimmy held me up. "Bobby, say hello to Rocket."

"Hi, Rocket. What brings you guys around? Is there anything I could do for a cute Chihuahua?"

Jimmy nodded. "Dean was telling me you might have an apartment available."

"It so happens that someone just moved out of 17 Deerhaunt Drive. Go up to my mom's house and tell her I sent you there. Tell her what you're looking for. I'm sure she could help. And don't forget to bring Rocket down sometime to see the horse, cows, and donkeys. Just bring her down anytime."

Next, we headed to see Bobby's mom. I overheard Dean telling Jimmy all about her. Her name was Tina, she was 86 years old, and she goes bungee jumping. The way they talked about it, that's a really big deal when you're 86 years old.

As Dean drove up the hill, all I could see were trees and a lot of birds. We stopped when we reached the top of the hill. The sign read "Deerhaunt Drive." I thought that had a nice sound to it.

As Dean made the turn, we went down, then up another hill. I felt like I was going deep in the woods, just like the day I was abandoned, and the boys chased me. It was a bad memory, but with Jimmy next to me, it didn't last long.

At the end of the road, there was this big house with a long driveway. At the beginning of the driveway, a sign read, "The Tina's Residence."

Dean parked his truck in front of it, and Jimmy pulled the car up behind him. "We're here," Dean said. "Let's go meet Tina. Bring Rocket, too."

Jimmy leaned his head down and whispered, "Okay, Rocket, be nice. Let's hope we get this apartment."

Dean rang the bell, and the strangest thing happened. Lights started to blink on and off all around us. I thought maybe he rang the wrong bell. Then he rang it again, and a loud ringing happened. That scared me.

A few minutes later, Dean said, "Jimmy, maybe she isn't home. Let's come back later."

Just as we started to walk away, a voice called out, "Who's there?"

"It's Dean and Jimmy, friends of Bobby's. Oh, and Rocket, too."

The door opened to reveal a slender, elderly woman wearing a long dress and a bright colored scarf around her head. "Jimmy and who?"

Jimmy held me up. "Hi, Tina. I'm Jimmy, and this is Rocket. We were hoping you have an apartment for rent for Rocket and me."

"Oh, you're looking for a place," Tina said, and looked over her glasses at me. "And oh, how cute that dog is. What kind of dog is she?" "She's a Chihuahua," Jimmy said.

"Oh, that's good. They're very good dogs. They're one-owner dogs. Very protective, and very devoted to their owners." She thought a moment, then said, "We might have something for you. Come this way. I'll get the keys."

When she went back inside, Jimmy and Dean shook hands. "Jimmy, whenever you need anything, just let me know." "That goes for me, too, Dean," Jimmy said.

"Ruff! Ruff! Ruff!"

They were still laughing when Tina came back with the keys.

"Okay, Jimmy and Rocket, let's go," she said, then turned to Dean. "Dean, could you take the truck around to Number 17, please? That's the red house over there. I'll walk with Jimmy and Rocket to the house."

"So, Jimmy, how long do you think you're going to stay?" she asked as we walked.

"I really don't know, Tina. I have a son. He lives in Croton." "Oh, that's nice. What's his name?"

"Jimmy. Same as me. I call him JJ. I moved from Maopac. I just wanted to be close to him."

"Oh, I understand. Well, here we are. It's upstairs."

As we walked into the house, Jimmy saw a door on the left side. Jimmy asked Tina who lived there. She said it was a guy by the name of Joe.

As we looked at the apartment, I heard Tina and Jimmy talking about all the things it had. A full kitchen. A small bathroom. A living room, and a small bedroom, enough room for a single bed. As Jimmy walked around, he would say things like, "Yes, my couch and table can go in here," and "Hey, this wall is a great spot to put my Titanic picture and the tiger picture."

I could still hear Jimmy and Tina talking, but I had already made up my mind when I looked out of the window and saw how much running-room there was around.

*This is it*, I thought.

After a while, I heard Jimmy say, "Bye, Tina, thanks for everything."

"Bye, Jimmy and Rocket. I hope you have a nice stay here." And of course,

I just had to say, "Ruff! Ruff! Ruff!"

"Don't bark, Rocket," Jimmy said.

"Oh, Jimmy," Tina said. "She's so cute. And that's what dogs do-they bark! All she's doing is saying goodbye."

I decided that I loved Tina, almost as much as I loved Jimmy!

As soon as Jimmy and I returned to Dean's truck, Dean asked, "Jimmy, you taking it?"

Before Jimmy could get anything out, this guy that was watching us from the front door said, "Welcome to Deerhaunt. My name is Joe, and I live downstairs. And who's that cutie you have?"

"Hello, Joe," Jimmy said. "I'm Jimmy, and this little cutie is Rocket."

Joe pointed at the apartment door and said, "So, are you taking it, Jimmy?"

Jimmy smiled. "I already took it."

"Great," Joe said. "Do you need a hand with anything?" "No, Joe, thanks anyway. We have it."

Joe nodded. "Great. Welcome to the area." He chuckled, then said, "If you need anything, you know where I am."

"Okay, Joe, thanks for everything."

Dean spoke up, "Okay, let's get the stuff out of the truck." Jimmy looked back at him. "Right. Sorry for holding you up." "No problem, Jimmy," Dean said, and smiled at Jimmy, then at me.

Jimmy and Dean started taking things out of the truck and bringing them upstairs. They were working hard, but Jimmy didn't have that worried look anymore, and that made me happy.

After they unloaded the truck, I heard Jimmy tell Dean, "I feel free here. There's so much room. And no more crazy Mrs. Lipsky to deal with."

Dean laughed and said, "I hate to run, but I have to. You take good care of yourself and Rocket. I'll see you guys soon."

# ROCKET & THE CONSTRUCTION WORKER

Jimmy let me run around outside for a while. It was great. There was a big open space that was surrounded by woods. But whenever I got near the woods, Jimmy called me back. That was okay, because the woods kind of reminded me of the woods where the boys chased me that day so long ago. When I got tired, I ran right into his arms.

He hugged me and said, "Rock, we're home now. *Really* home. Now you can run all around as much as you like. Let's go upstairs and look at the apartment."

On the way up the stairs, I looked around. We lived in the only house up here. The rest of the houses around us look like trailer homes. All nice, and with nice yards. But of course! There's so much space around this place, it's like a field instead of a yard.

When we got back inside, I noticed something that I didn't notice before. All the windows in the house were low. Much easier for me to look out of than a regular window. I still had to jump really hard to see out of them, but not as much as in the old place.

Jimmy was quiet a while, staring at me, then the window. Then he said, "Rocket, how about if I make you an elevator?"

"Hey, that's great," I barked. "I can look out anytime I want!" But it seemed he had a different idea. "See this window?" he said. "This one leads out onto the stairway. The one just above the porch roof."

I'd seen that on one of my many jumps. There was a staircase that led from the attic of the house, and the porch roof was right below it.

"If I put an elevator there," he continued, "and put papers or something on the porch roof, whenever you wanted to go out, all you'd have to do is hop in the cage and press the down button, then hop out, do your business, and when you're done, hop back and come back in the very same way. How's that sound?"

I wanted to tell him that I didn't think it was a good idea, but I couldn't talk, of course. So when he asked me again, I just walked away.

"So you don't like my idea?" he said. "Okay, say no more, I get it now. I was only thinking of you."

"Ruff! Ruff!"

He laughed. "Oh, so you *do* talk. Love you, Rocket." "Ruff! Ruff!"

"Yeah, I know you do, too."

I went over to him and licked his face, loving him for understanding. Yet later on, I wished I'd told him yes about the elevator. But that's further on in the story, and I don't want to get ahead of myself.

The rest of the night, Jimmy was putting his things away, moving things around, trying them this way and that way. He also spent some time on cleaning, and when he finished, everything sparkled. After a while, he turned to me and said, "Okay, Rock, I'm tired of work. Let's go out for a bit."

He put my leash on, and we left. It was really dark outside at first, but soon, the moon came out, and the stars. Plenty of light to see by. Jimmy sat on the grass, looked up, then lay back, and I lay right beside him.

"Rocket," he said. "There's a shooting star. Remember what I said about them?"

Sure I did. When you see a shooting star you make a wish, and the wish will come true. So even though I had everything I ever wished for right here, I made a wish anyway-that we would always be free of people like Mrs.

Lipsky, who wouldn't let us be free.

## CHAPTER 9

# Rocket Meets Squeaky Again

"After a while, Jimmy said, "Well, it's getting late. Let's go up." He stood, picked me up and started walking toward the house.

I saw something moving fast, and I jumped out of his arms and started to run after it. I could hear Jimmy calling me, "No! Rocket, come here, Rock!"

I slowed down and looked back at Jimmy, trying to figure out why he seemed so excited. Then I looked back, and I saw it-it was a raccoon, running into the woods and out of sight.

When I got back to Jimmy, he didn't seem happy. "No, no," he said. "You never jump out of my arms like that again. Do you hear me? Never! That was a raccoon, and you don't want to tangle with them."

I only kept my head down while he was talking. But when he finished, I looked up at him, remembering how Dad and the boys used to yell at me. I couldn't help it; I whimpered at the memory.

"Rocket, I'm so sorry for yelling at you," Jimmy said, his voice shaking a little. "But please . . . *please*, Rocket, don't do that any more."

He picked me up and kissed my head. I felt okay after that. He wasn't yelling because he hated me, just that he was scared for me. That's when I learned that there's a big difference between mean yelling, and scared yelling.

Back inside the apartment, Jimmy said, "Rocket, I had a long day. I'm going to get some sleep. I'll put your bed right over here, okay?"

"Ruff!"

While Jimmy checked the alarm clock and put the light out, I put my head down on my blanket, looked out of the window, and started to remember all my friends at the Humane Society. I wondered if King and Prince were doing all right. And that little Golden Lab that use to cuddle in my stomach. Gail, Terry, and Lisa; George, Victor and Johnny; and Dr. Casey. Oh, I can't forget my friends Tom and his wife.

*Oh, what's that?* I thought. *Is that a tear from my eye?* But it wasn't because I was sad. Sure, I miss all the humans and animals at the Humane Society. But I was really happy because I had a chance in my life to meet friends like that. I'm sure they were all doing fine.

Jimmy's alarm clock got me going, and soon Jimmy was getting up.

"Morning, Rocket, want to go bye-bye?"

I wiggled my tail, stood on my hind legs and showed my teeth.

He laughed. "I'll take that as a yes. Okay, let's go."

We went downstairs, Jimmy opened the door, and I flew out of the door and started to run. I saw a squirrel jumping from tree to tree, and decided to give tree jumping another try. But just like before, I fell right on my back. "Keep on trying," I heard the squirrel say. "You never know." Seemed like I'd heard that before.

I barked at the squirrel.

"Rocket, come here," Jimmy said. "I have to get to work."

As I was running back to him, he looked up at the squirrel and said, "Bye, squirrel, see you again!"

"Squeaky," I heard the squirrel call back. "Call me Squeaky." I stopped so fast, I did a forward flip.

As soon as I could get back on my feet, I yelled, "Squeaky? Squeaky, is that really you?"

"Yes, it is," Squeaky said. "Hey, haven't I seen you somewhere before?"

"It's Sweeney. Remember, Sweeney?" "Sweeney from where?"

Jimmy knew something strange was happening, but I was so shocked I couldn't even bark at him. "What do we have here?" he said. "A squirrel and a dog jumping together? Rocket, you'll have to play later. We've got to go." He scooped me up and started walking back to the house.

"Squeaky, it's Sweeney!" I yelled back. "My name's Rocket now, but I was Sweeney when we met before. Remember? The woods when they left me there, remember? You told me to keep an eye out for King!"

"Rocket, come on, quit that barking," Jimmy said.

I ignored him. "Squeaky, hang around," I barked. "As soon as I get back, we'll talk. I've got lots to tell you!"

Squeaky waved, said, "Sure!" and then hopped into the trees.

"I don't believe this," I said. "I love Squeaky, and she's here!"

Sure, sometimes humans can read minds, but this time, Jimmy completely missed the boat. "Rocket, I don't know what it is with dogs and squirrels, but you definitely get excited when you see them. You just be careful whenever you're outside, okay?"

I wanted to tell him that squirrels aren't like raccoons, but maybe he would figure that out in time.

When we got back to the house, Jimmy and I said our goodbyes, and he told me to hold down the fort. I didn't know what a fort is, but I figured it had something to do with guarding the house-which I always did anyway. So I gave him a "Ruff!" and he left, whistling a happy song.

As soon as he closed the door, I raced to the window. And there she was, looking at me from the tree by the house. I barked and barked, she jumped, and I knew I had a good friend in her. I was so happy, I wanted to cry.

I looked around the apartment, then out of the window. Squeaky was gone, doing her thing. Whatever that was. Probably looking for nuts. There were a lot of them around. How she got to these parts of the woods beats me. It had to be miles away from where I first met her. From tree to tree, maybe? Man, why didn't I say yes when Jimmy offered to build me that elevator? I could have gone outside and looked for her! Oh, well, like I've heard Jimmy say, that's water under the bridge.

I wished I could jump like she did. I jump high, but she can jump from tree to tree, just like that! But I think it's good that we all have different abilities. Some jump high, some jump far, some hop, some swim, some fly, some crawl . . . whatever we do, we all live together to be a success in life. One success is to be happy.

Anyway, Squeaky knew I was here, and I can talk to her again tonight.

I got through the day, and even though I went to the window many times, I didn't see Squeaky again. It was getting late now, and I wondered what time Jimmy was coming back. I had to go to the bathroom, and try to find Squeaky. And if it got dark, I didn't know if I could see Squeaky. I didn't know what squirrels do when it gets dark.

The only odd thing that happened was that, once or twice, I heard someone come up to the door, knock, and then walk away. It was a soft knock, so I only barked a couple of times each time it happened. Didn't sound too threatening. To be honest, I got a good feeling each time it happened.

It started to get dark, really dark. But a little moonlight came through the window, so that was good.

I heard a car coming. Hey, it sounded like Jimmy's! I hoped it was. The walk down the hallway seemed forever when I had to go.

I heard the key rattling in the door, and then Jimmy came in!

"Hi, Rocket," he said. "How was your first day alone in your new apartment?"

"Ruff! Ruff! Ruff!" I said, then ran toward the door.

## ROCKET & THE CONSTRUCTION WORKER

"Oh, yeah, I guess you need to go outside. Okay, give me a minute."

It was a long minute, but I was glad he got the hint. As he opened the door, I bolted down the stairs, only to be blocked by another door-the one I forgot about.

When he opened the second door, I was flying. I did my business, and ran around and around. It was great to be outside.

"Get out of here!" I heard Jimmy yell.

I turned around to see him throwing rocks at a raccoon. "Ruff! Ruff! Ruff!" I shouted, and started running toward it. "No, Rocket, let it go!" I heard him yell as I ran.

I didn't stop running until it disappeared.

I didn't have a clue where it went, maybe up a tree. I thought about searching for it, but I heard Jimmy calling me, so I started walking back toward the house. Jimmy, looking all frantic, called out, "Rocket, you don't want to fight with a raccoon. They're crazy, and they carry rabies."

When I got close enough, he smiled at me, picked me up and kissed me on the head. "You were trying to protect me, weren't you? Thanks anyway, Rock, I love you."

We walked back into the house, him holding me in his arms. He put me down inside. "Oh, Rocket, it's nice to be home. Did you have a good day?

Hope so."

I wanted to tell him so much. That I looked and looked all day, but didn't see Squeaky. And that I heard someone outside the door earlier. But all I could do was bark, and lick his hands and face. For now, that seemed like enough.

Again, that soft, gentle knock came at the door.

"Who's there?" Jimmy said.

"It's me, Jimmy. Tina."

"Hello, Tina. What a nice surprise."

"Jimmy, I came by earlier. I wanted to tell you when you walk your dogOh, my, she's such a cutie!" "Ruff! Ruff! Ruff!"

"No, Rock, be good!" Jimmy said. Then he turned back to Tina. "Yes, Jimmy. Could you keep her on a leash when you're near the buildings? You can let her run as around the big area, but outside of that, keep her on a leash." "Sure, Tina. No problem."

"Thanks, Jimmy. Bye, Rocky. Oh, excuse me, it's Rocket. Bye, Rocket!"

"Ruff! Ruff! Ruff!"

As she walked down the hall toward the stairs, the sounds were familiar. Yes, it *was* Tina that I heard outside the door earlier. That was good to know. She was a sweet old lady. I'd never be afraid of her, like I was of Mrs. Lipsky. And I was sure she would never do anything mean to Jimmy or me.

Jimmy closed the door, gave me a wink and said, "Good girl."

I went over to my blanket and lay down, thinking how much I loved my life. I thought I would never feel this way, but I had faith. It's good to have faith. It gives you hope for a better life.

Jimmy started to do a few things in the house, and I went back to the window. The moon was out now, and just as I saw Squeaky in a tree, I saw something moving down in the big area. At first, I thought the raccoon had come back. But it was even worse. It was a fox, and it was trying to get up the tree and get Squeaky!

The fox started to go up the tree. Squeaky wasn't moving. I don't even think she saw it coming at her!

I barked, and Jimmy came to the window, saw the fox, opened the window and yelled, "Get out of here. Get out!"

Squeaky heard Jimmy, turned around, saw the fox, and jumped from tree to tree until she was gone. The fox didn't run, just stared at Jimmy and me.

"Go on, get out of here, Go on!" Jimmy shouted. A moment later, he turned to me. "It's all right now, Rock. She's gone."

I whimpered. Yes, the fox was gone, but Squeaky was too!

Sighing, Jimmy knelt down next to me. "Rocket, I'm sorry, but I'm not letting you run around here on your own. If we've got foxes . . . they're bad and tough. Tougher then the raccoons you were chasing. I'd hate to see you tangle with one. So no running around in the big area at night. In the daytime, they hide. It's at night they roam."

What could I say to that? "Ruff! Ruff!" But I didn't say it loud.

While Jimmy got ready for bed, I looked through the window. I could see Squeaky! But this time, she was on the tree right outside the window. She waved at me, and I put my paws on the window and barked "Goodnight, my friend. I'll see you tomorrow. Be careful!"

She waved and left, and I lay down on my blanket, happy and excited about what just happened. Even though there were some dangers here, this was going to be an exciting place to live.

Jimmy was about to turn in, but he called to me.

"Rocket, the job I'm working on now is in the city. I hope I won't be too late every day, but I never know. So if you have to go to the bathroom while I'm gone, here's how to do it."

He took me into the bathroom, where he had laid out some newspapers. "If you have to go, go on those papers, okay?"

I licked his face. Now, I wouldn't have to wait anymore!

"Good girl," he said, and chuckled. I guess my licks tickle him.

"I'm going to get some sleep now. And you do, too."

He put me down, and I went right for my blanket. He turned off all the lights except for my nightlight, set his alarm clock, and went to his bed. A minute later, I heard him breathing like he was asleep. I looked at the moonlight coming in the windows and took a deep breath. It was so quiet, so peaceful, and I just knew the rest of my life would be as happy as I was right then.

I guess I was asleep when I hear the sound. It was someone calling my name really soft: "Rocket! Rocket!" But it wasn't Jimmy's voice, or Tina's.

I opened my eyes, and saw Squeaky in the window. I got out of my bed, quietly to keep from waking Jimmy up, and headed over there.

"Hi, Squeaky," I said, keeping my voice low. "How you're doing? That was a close one with the fox."

"Yeah, I know. I just wanted to come over and thank you for waking me up. That fox has been after me since I got here."

"Yeah?"

"Yeah, she's tough. So be careful whenever you're outside."
"Will do, Squeaky."

"So how are things going for you?" she asked, then glanced at Jimmy's sleeping form. "Is he nice?"

"Squeaky, I could just write a book about how nice he is," I said. "Someday, I'll tell you all about how we met. But right now, I want to ask . . . have you seen or heard about King?"

She shook her head. "I saw one of his gang once, before I came here. But he didn't know anything."

I told her that King had been adopted from the Humane Society, and she was glad.

"I've known King a long time, and he's a very independent dog," she said. "But deep down, I always thought he'd be happy if he had the right kind of human home."

"And there's something else I want to talk about, too," I said. "I want to find a way to get rid of that fox."

She looked confused. "What do you mean, Rocket? How can we get rid of a fox?"

"Well, I know there's a raccoon in the woods, and that's kind of bad, but Jimmy told me that a fox is lots worse. And it's already tried to get at you and hurt you. So if that fox won't join us, and she keeps chasing you, she has to go."

"How on earth are we going to get rid of a fox?"

"I haven't thought of a way yet," I told her. "But leave it up to me, Squeaky my friend. I'll think of something."

"Whatever you say, Rocket," she said, and smiled. "I've got to go for now. Goodnight."

"Goodnight, Squeaky. And make sure you go very high in the tree . . . at least until I come up with a plan."

She nodded, and disappeared into the darkness.

I lay down on my blanket, and the next thing I remember is Jimmy getting up and ready for work. He took me outside and I ran around. I looked for Squeaky, but maybe she was still asleep. It was still pretty early.

Right before he left, Jimmy said, "Now remember, I'll be back as soon as I can, but I might be late. You have food and plenty of

## ROCKET & THE CONSTRUCTION WORKER

water, like usual. And if I'm not home in time, you know what to do if you have to go."

I watched him open the door to his car, and watched while he drove away. And then, I went back to my bed and started thinking about Squeaky and the fox, and trying to think of a plan. A good plan didn't come to me, but the more I thought about it, the madder I got. *That fox has to go,* I thought. *It's got everyone scared, and even Jimmy is nervous about it. And Squeaky and her friends are in danger. Something has to be done, and soon.*

Still, I didn't know what to do about it. I could fight her, but I didn't want to hurt her. And what if I did end up hurting her? Maybe other foxes would come, and I couldn't fight all of them. But if not fighting her, what could I do? Foxes are hard to trick.

Some time went by. I don't know how long, but it started to get dark. I had to go, and thought about going to see the paper. But, I decided to try and hold it.

Just as I made that decision, I heard a car. Yep, it was Jimmy!

Before we left to go outside, Jimmy smacked his forehead. "Oh, I forgot about the leash. Come here, and let's put it on. Especially with that fox around."

The fox. Always the fox.

As Jimmy walked with me around the house, I saw two of Squeaky's friends. They were digging in the dirt, probably hiding their nuts. Whatever they were doing, they looked cute.

"Wait a minute. That's it!" I barked.

Jimmy misunderstood. "So you like here, Rocket? Is that what you're saying?"

"Ruff! Ruff! Ruff!" "I'm glad you do."

If Jimmy only knew what I was really thinking about, I don't know if he'd like it. Well, maybe he would. He doesn't like that fox anyway. But now, I had an idea, and I couldn't wait to share it with Squeaky.

"Okay, Rocket, ready to go back?"

I looked around, kinda whimpered, then stood on my hind legs to reach up to him.

"Oh, you want me to carry you? Okay, up!" I jumped right into his arms.

"What, the fox got you scared? Don't worry about it I'll take care of it." *Jimmy, if my plan works, you won't have to.*

He let me down at the door, and I ran upstairs faster than he did. As soon as we were inside the apartment, I ran to the window to see if I could see Squeaky. She wasn't there.

We had dinner, watched a little TV. Jimmy had some reports to do, and he seemed kind of tired. Finally, he placed some papers into a big envelope, and reached his arms over his head and stretched. "Hey, Rocket, I'm going to turn in. I'm beat. You coming?" I just sat there.

"Okay, see you in the morning, then."

Jimmy went to bed. A few minutes later, Squeaky came to the window, and I told her my plan.

"We don't want to hurt her," I said, "we just want her to leave us alone. Why don't we dig a big hole, and cover it up to disguise it? When she steps on it, she'll fall in."

Squeaky looked at me funny. "Okay, I can see digging a hole. You're a dog. You dig holes. I'm a squirrel. I dig holes. And I've got maybe twenty or thirty friends who can help. But how are we going to cover the hole? Cover it with what?"

Oh, man, I hadn't thought of that. I looked around and saw my blanket. I pointed to it and said. "Look over there. It's a big blanket."

She peered in the window. The nightlight gave just enough light for her to see it. "Okay, that might work. *If* you can get it out of there."

"Don't worry about that. I'll take care of it." At that moment, I had no idea, but remember, Chihuahuas are confident.

"Okay," Squeaky said, "how big a hole do you think we'll need?"

I thought a moment. "Well, the fox isn't very big. Maybe two feet deep by two feet wide?"

She considered that, and finally nodded. "But that might take a long time."

"Well, how long has the fox been here?"

She sighed in frustration. "That fox was here when we got here."

"Oh? So you moved right in on the fox?"

"Well, I guess you could call it that. But we don't want to hurt the fox, we just want to talk to her. Convince her to leave us alone. Right?"

"Yeah, that's all we want to do. And it might take a while to dig the hole, but that's okay. Talk to your crew, and let me know when we'll start."

She nodded. "Sure, Rocket."

"Okay, Squeaky. I have to go to bed now, but I'll see you later. I'll look for you tomorrow. If you don't see me outside, come here at night, okay? Maybe on the roof."

She nodded, waved, and left.

I spent the few minutes before I went to sleep trying to figure out a way to get the blanket outside when it was time to scare the fox. Nothing came to me, but I figured that if I had faith, I'd figure it out in time.

# CHAPTER 10

# The Capture Of The Fox

I didn't see Squeaky from the window the next day, so I just figured she was talking to all her friends. With thirty friends, that's a lot of talking. I didn't see her when Jimmy and I went outside, either. But I did see something else interesting. Very interesting.

Jimmy and I were walking right next to the woods when Jimmy said, "Look there, Rocket, somebody must have picnics here."

I looked, and saw a great big piece of cloth. It had blue and white squares on it, like a tablecloth I saw once in the House of Misery. Thinking about that place made me shudder, but I got over it fast. Why? Because the problem of what to cover the hole with was solved!

It was partly covered with leaves, but that was okay. In fact, that might be why no one ever noticed it before and returned it to their owners. More and more, I believed that faith could really make things happen.

There was a tree right next to the cloth. I ran over there and scratched it with my teeth to mark it. I figured that, in the dark, that would help the squirrels to see it.

"Hey, girl, you must be hungry," Jimmy said. "Don't eat the tree bark.

Let's go have dinner instead."

Well, I *was* hungry. But even more than that, I was hungry to catch a fox!

As soon as dinner was over, Jimmy said, "Hey, Rocket, let's look at the stars for a while. I hope we see a shooting one. If we do, I'll make a wish to be on this job for a long time. Construction has its ups and downs. The ups outweigh the downs, big time. And I really like this job." He looked at me and scratched behind my ears. "So, did you have a good day today? Run into any of your friends today?"

"Ruff! Ruff!"

"You like it here?" "Ruff!"

"Good. Sometimes, Rocket, I think you know exactly what I'm taking about."

That would be a true statement. But hey, how could he possibly know that I understand every word he says? I went over to him and he rubbed my head with his hand. I licked it all over. A minute later, he went to the kitchen to get something to drink and some crackers.

Oh, and one of those bones for my snack. I love the bones he gives me.

They're the best. Yum!

We just relaxed for a while, until he noticed movement in the trees.

"Hey, Rock," he whispered, "I think that's your friend, the fox." I pretended to ignore him, hoping he would get sleepy soon. Finally, Jimmy said, "Rocket, I'm going to turn in. It's almost eleven o'clock."

When he lay down in his bed, I went to my bed too. Wow. I didn't think I was so tired. I rested my head on the blanket. The next thing I heard was tapping on the window. I tried to open my eyes, but I couldn't. I felt something poking me in the back. I moved around a little and opened my eyes, scared-until I saw what was poking me in the back.

"Squeaky," I whispered. "What are you doing here? How did you get inside?"

"Weren't we supposed to meet on the roof?"

"Oh, no. I was so tired. I guess I fell asleep. I'm sorry."

"That's all right, Rocket. Everyone's still here. Let's go on the roof."

"Okay, but where are you going? That's Jimmy's room." Squeaky grinned.

"That's the way I came in. He leaves his window open a little."

"Okay, let's go. But be quiet."

Actually, Jimmy left his window open a lot. It was easy for me to squeeze through after Squeaky.

The other squirrels were sitting quietly on the roof, with barely a chatter. "All right!" I said. "Hey guys, how are you doing?" Just light chattering.

"Okay, here's something I need to teach you about. I know that squirrels chatter, but that's not a good idea here. My owner might wake up and hear you. So when you agree with something I say, here's what to do."

I showed them a human nod. And they did a pretty good job of it.

"Okay, that means yes. And when you want to say no, shake your head from side to side, like this." I demonstrated, and they did great.

I turned to Squeaky. "Squeaky, over here. There's a few things I need to go over with you."

"Hi, Rocket," one of the squirrels said. "Hi," I replied. "What's your name?" "They call me Nuts. MickeyNuts."

"Glad to meet you, MickeyNuts. Okay, let's get a little closer. I don't want my owner to hear us. Squeaky, you know where you stay? Between the two trees over there. The fox knows you're there a lot, and she'll be hoping to catch you there. She was there today."

I looked around at the group. "I'm sure Squeaky told you about my plan. So my question is: How long do you think it'll take you to dig a hole two feet deep and two feet wide?"

# ROCKET & THE CONSTRUCTION WORKER

They all looked at each other, chattering softly. Then MickeyNuts turned to me and said, "Maybe two or four." "What?" I said. "Days?"

"No, Rocket. With the digging and spreading the dirt, maybe five hours."

"Five *hours?*"

I looked at the other members of the group, and they were all nodding.

"So, when do you want us to get started?" Squeaky asked.

"As soon as possible. But you have to be careful. As long as you're on the ground, digging, you'll be easy for her to see. So post plenty of lookouts." They all nodded at that.

I looked at the trees. "Okay, guys, do you see the two trees over there?" Nods all around.

"Just between those trees, you start digging. When I went down there today, I made a mark on one of the tree. You'll see something there that looks like a blanket. It's got kind of blue and white marks on it. When you finish with the hole, put the blue thing over it, and then cover it with grass and leaves. Not too much . . . we don't want it to fall in. And put some dirt on each of the four corners to hold it on." I turned to Squeaky. "Squeaky what do think?"

"I think it's going to work, Rocket. How lucky you were to find that cloth!"

I nodded. "That's because I had faith." "Faith? What's that?"

I remembered Lady asking me that question, so long ago, and I smiled. "Like I told a friend of mine, it's the same thing as confidence." I looked at the group and said, "So there you have it, folks."

"We got it, Rocket," MickeyNuts said. "I have a few things I'd like to say to that fox. When she falls in, we're all going to surrounds the hole and give her a peace of our mind."

"Hey, Rocket." "Yeah, Squeaky?"

"How you going to get down when you're watching from the window?

Hmmm. I hadn't really thought about that yet. "Okay guys. I'll tell you. In life, we all have great qualities. My quality is that I can jump high, *real* high if I want." I pointed to the staircase that went over the porch, just above our heads. I'll just jump onto that, and head down the staircase."

Squeaky looked doubtful. "I don't know, Rocket. That's an awfully high jump."

I have them all a smile. "Guys, you just don't know what you can accomplish when you have faith!"

"Okay, Rocket," Squeaky said, laughing. "We'll get right on it tomorrow."

"Sounds good. See you guys tomorrow."

They all climbed down off the roof, and I climbed back through Jimmy's window. Jimmy was moving around a bit, but he was still sound asleep. I went over to my blanket and rested my head on my paws. In seconds, I was back in dreamland.

The next thing I heard was Jimmy's alarm clock going off.

Wow, I must have been *really* tired!

And actually, I was still tired from my late night. I could see him reach over and shut the alarm off, and I closed my eyes-until he said, "You know, it's funny, Rocket. I hardly ever dream. But last night, I dreamed about squirrels. And they were all making funny noises."

I opened my eyes, did my best to give him an innocent look, stood on my hind legs and wiggled my tail. Them he said the magic words: "Rocket, want to go outside?" Well, sure!

Jimmy noticed that I was tired, so when we got downstairs, he said, "Let's just walk around the cul-de-sac today. I've been wanting to check out the area around the trailers, anyway."

After he left, I went to my blanket. I could hear the car starting up. I was so tired, I closed my eyes for a minute.

"Hello, hello, hello, Rocket," I heard at the window. "It's Squeaky. Rocket, are you there?"

"Oh, hi, Squeaky. Hi, MickeyNuts. I must have fallen asleep. What time is it?"

MickeyNuts said, "The sun is right overhead."

Sure enough, it was. "Noon," I said. "We have to get started." MickeyNuts laughed. "We already started."

I looked toward the two trees, and there was already a big pile of dirt there. The hole was well underway. And it looked like a little army was down there, working away.

"Come on," Squeaky said. "Let's go down. You can help us dig."

"Better not, guys," I told them. "I don't want Tina to see me downstairs in the daytime. She'll tell Jimmy, and then I'm in trouble. But the hole looks good." I looked at MickeyNuts. "Don't forget the blue cover, and to cover it with leaves."

"Great. When it's done, let me know. And make sure if you see Tina, to hide. Tina is the old lady that walks around here."

Squeaky nodded. "She already came by twice, and we hid. It's cool. We'll still be done in no time."

"I hope so," MickeyNuts said. "I'm tired of that fox. I can't wait to get her. Squeaky, she falls in the hole, then we talk. Right?"

I yawned, and that startled both squirrels. "Guys, I'm gonna have to get some rest. Check with me later, okay?"

"Sure, Rocket. MickeyNuts and I have to get back to the crew anyway. See ya later!"

The minute they left, I went to my blanket and closed my eyes. The next thing I heard was Jimmy walking up the stairs. *Oh, I wonder if they finished with the hole,* I thought. I raced over to the window. Wow! It looked they finished it. And the squirrels were still all there. When they saw me, they waved. I put my two front paws up on the window to let them I'd seen them, and what a fine job they did.

I heard the door open, and Jimmy say, "Hi, Rocket. Let me unwind a bit, and I'll take you out. How was your day? Anything exciting happen?"

*Oh, nothing much,* I wanted to tell him. *I just directed a bunch of squirrels to dig a hole for the fox and cover it up to look like nothing happened. That exciting enough for ya?*

But of course, I couldn't.

Jimmy put my leash on and we went outside. Of course, I was careful to avoid that area. Didn't want Jimmy to wonder what was going on.

"Okay, Rocket," he said after a few minutes. "Let's make it back. I have to go out tonight to a party. Don't want to be late, and I have to get ready."

We had dinner, he took a shower and got dressed. As he was leaving, he said the usual: "Watch the fort, Rocket." "Ruff! Ruff! Ruff!" *You better believe I will!*

I could hear the car starting up and driving away. Then there was silence. I wasn't sleepy yet, so I got up and wandered to the window. The stars . . . there were so many of them. The sky was *filled* with stars. Then I looked down and saw the raccoon. And it was *way* too close to the hole.

I had to distract it. I scanned the trees, but didn't see Squeaky. She could be a decoy, but she wasn't there. So I did the only other thing I could think of . . .

"Ruff! Ruff! Ruff! Ruff!"

The raccoon ran the other way. Whew! That was close.

After a while, I got sleepy and went to bed. The next thing I heard was keys rattling in the door. Jimmy was back from the party.

I lifted my head to say hello to him.

"Hello, Rocket," he said. "How you doing, my cutie? Want to go out?"

It was awfully late, but hey, I'll never turn down a chance to go out. But I had to make sure to keep Jimmy distracted. It wouldn't do for him to see that the blue cloth wasn't where it was before.

Everything went fine until we were headed back to the house.

# ROCKET & THE CONSTRUCTION WORKER

Then Jimmy said, "Rocket, what's that?"

And he was staring directly at the blue cloth!

Just as he started to walk toward it, but I started whimpering, acting scared.

"What's wrong, Rocket?" He looked around. "Do you see that fox? . . . Yeah, guess it *is* kind of late to be out."

He gave the cloth one last glance, then said, "Maybe some kids were out here playing, and moved it. I'll check it out tomorrow when the light's better.

Come on Rocket, time for bed."

Wow, that was a closer one than the raccoon!

I wasn't too worried about tomorrow. Tomorrow, the fox is coming back, and we'll be ready for her. And even if Jimmy sees the hole, maybe he'll think some kids did that, too.

Inside, Jimmy undressed for bed. When he took his shirt off, a smell came over me. I didn't know the smell, but it was familiar to me somehow.

He picked me up and we both looked up at the sky, then he kissed me on the head. I sniffed him, trying to remember where I had smelled that smell before.

"Rocket, what are you doing?" He thought a moment, then said, "Yeah, I was around a lot of people. . . . and I met this girl. With a little luck, you'll meet her someday."

When I woke up, Jimmy's alarm was going off, but he didn't wake up right away. He was working a lot, even on weekends, and coming home late. But once, I heard him say to JJ that he had to take the overtime while it's there. Whatever it means, it means he's gone a lot more.

This morning, our walk took us by Tina's house again. She was there like clockwork, watering her flowers.

When she saw us, she waved. "Oh, Jimmy," she said, "I have something for you."

Jimmy greeted her and walked over to stand next to her.

"I found out something," she said. "Do you know what 'Chihuahua' means?"

Jimmy looked down at me and smiled. "No, I don't Tina. Love, maybe?"

She laughed, then said, "No. It's Mexican. It means a Mexican guard dog. And just like I thought, they're one-master dogs. They only listen to one person."

Jimmy thanked her, and we left to head back to our apartment. I think Tina's a very nice old lady. I know she likes me.

Just before we walked up to the door, I noticed something moving behind the trees. It was the fox!

I had to call Squeaky, but I had to be careful about it; if I started barking now, Jimmy would wonder why. And if he saw the fox, he might chase it. If he did that, he might fall into the hole!

Jimmy opened the door, and I went straight for the window.

"Rocket, what are you doing? Come here, give me a kiss goodbye."

I went over to Jimmy he picked me up, kissed me on the head, and said, "Hope I'm not too late. But if I am, there's plenty of water and dry food for you. And if you have to go, you know where to go. Okay, Rock, see you later. Hold the fort down." *I will, Jimmy! You better believe it!*

The minute he closed the door, I ran to the window. As soon as I saw Jimmy drive away, I barked to see if Squeaky was nearby. She was.

"Squeaky, the fox is back," I said quickly. "I saw her."

Squeaky nodded. "Okay, I'll get the guys, and then I'll go lay down on the rock by the hole."

When I looked at her, confused, she shrugged. "Somebody's got to be a decoy. I'm the fastest."

# ROCKET & THE CONSTRUCTION WORKER

I nodded. "Well, you'd better hurry and get in position, then."
"Wait a minute."
"Yeah, Squeaky?"
"Suppose she jumps over the hole . . . I'm a goner, right?"
"She's not going to jump. She never jumps."
"Hummm."

I saw Squeaky jumping from tree to tree, telling the others as she went that I'd seen the fox, and everyone needed to be alert.

Soon, the crew was in position in the trees, and Squeaky was resting on the rock, casually looking around.

A little time went by, and Squeaky pretended to be asleep.

I could see the fox, creeping slowly, slowly to where Squeaky lay. I held my breath and glanced at the trees. The crew must have seen her too; nobody moved.

The fox stopped, almost right at the edge of the hole, and picked up her foreleg She was about to step onto the blue cloth!

Squeaky was just on the other side of the cloth, and the temptation must have been irresistible. But she didn't take the step. Instead, she looked back to see if anyone was coming. I could see her mouth, with those razor sharp teeth, dripping with saliva.

Just when I didn't think I could take it anymore, the fox's head whipped around, and with her eyes glued on Squeaky, she took a step, and fell into the hole!

Everyone started yelling, "We got the fox! We got her!"

I raced into Jimmy's room, squeezed through the slightly open window, jumped onto the porch roof, jumped onto the steps and raced down them.

"Good job, guys," I panted when I got to the hole. "You're the best!"

"Well, you're a great jumper," Squeaky said, laughing. "I was worried that you couldn't jump to those stairs, but you didn't even hesitate!"

"Hey, you're right!" I said. "But that's what faith will do!"

We looked down into the hole. The fox was in there, trembling and looking terrified.

"Hey, Fox," I said, "You like scaring us, don't you?"

"No-No, I don't," the fox said. Its voice was shaking.

"Well, it seems like you do. It seems like you can't wait to scare us. You looked like you couldn't wait to have Squeaky in your mouth." "Well . . . I'm sorry."

"Sorry? Ha! We can't even enjoy the place where we live because of you. My owner won't even let me off the leash because of you. Squeaky and her family and friends can't even run around because of you. Like, when is it going to stop? I know you have a big family, and we don't want any trouble. But this has to stop. So, Fox, do you have any suggestions?"

The fox was quiet, and from the look in her eyes, I could tell that she wasn't trying to figure out a way for us to live together. Nope, I think she was trying to figure out a way to get out of that hole, and have all of us for supper!"

"Look," I said. "Either you join us, or you leave us alone, or we leave you in the hole. And if you ever get out of the hole, you should tell your family about this."

"Yeah," Squeaky said. "If you don't leave us alone, you and your family might fall in holes all day and every day. *If* you know what I mean."

MickeyNuts was so angry, he picked up some dirt and threw it into the hole. As he started to pick up some more, Squeaky said, "No, MickeyNuts.

No throwing dirt on the fox. At least, not yet." Then she looked down in the hole. "Well, Fox? What do you say?"

The fox turned around in the hole to look at all of us. "Okay, okay! I'm sorry. I won't bother you guys anymore. And I'm sorry I scared you." I glared at her, trying to decide if she meant what she said.

"What's your name?" "My name is Candy."

"Well, I'm Rocket. And this is Squeaky. Guys, introduce yourselves."

One by one, the others called out their names. When they finished, I turned back to Candy. "Okay, Candy, you gave your word."

"I sure did. And foxes never go back on their word."

Even though foxes are known for their sneaky behavior, somehow, I believed her.

Part of the cloth had fallen into the hole with Candy. So I grabbed one end of it, then nodded to the others. "Okay, we're going to pull you up. Grab onto the other end of this cloth, as tight as you can."

"Okay, Rocket."

I looked at the others. "Okay, guys, let's do it. Candy, watch for dirt falling down onto you. And on three, we'll begin pulling."

The minute we got her level with the top of the hole, Candy leaped out of it, growling and showing her teeth.

The squirrels scrambled away, but Squeaky stayed by my side.

I growled and show my teeth to Candy. "So, what you going to do? You have a choice. You can do what you promised, or you and I can end it right here. Either way, you're never going to bother me and my friends again."

It was quiet for a while, and I wondered if I would really have to fight to defend my home, and my friends.

But thankfully, Candy decided to keep her word. "Okay, guys," she said. "You must know how hard it is for any animal to go against their instincts. But . . . I've watched you guys for a long time, and I think you're special. I like to think I'm special, too. So when I said that I wouldn't scare you guys anymore, I meant it. And I'll tell my family to leave you alone, too."

Finally, I was able to relax. But still, I warned her, "Look, I'm more than willing to be your friend. And Squeaky and the other squirrels feel the same way. If you don't try to hurt or scare us, we won't try to hurt or scare you. But you have to keep your end of the bargain, okay?"

Candy nodded, then said, "I really, truly mean it. And," she glanced at the hole, "thank you for helping me get out of the hole. You guys won't get any more trouble out of me. If I see you in the woods, I'll either ignore you, or call out to let you know I'm here. That's all."

I nodded. "That's good enough for me. That way, we can all live here together, and none of us have to be scared anymore."

The squirrels nodded, and Candy did, too. Then she started walking away. "Hey, Candy," I said.

She turned around, and her eyes looked suspicious.

I smiled at her. "Don't be a stranger."

She gave us a friendly, *non*-scary smile. And when a fox smiles like that, it's a beautiful thing!

Still smiling, she walked away, and I turned to walk back to the house. Squeaky and the others were cheering me on, yelling, "Yeah for Rocket!

Yeah for Rocket!" It reminded me of the days at the Humane Society, where I had learned so much about getting along with others, and about standing up for myself and those I love.

It wasn't as hard to get back into Jimmy's room as I thought. The staircase made a natural ladder almost all the way to the porch. It only took one big jump to make it from the staircase to the porch, and another one from the porch back to Jimmy's window.

Just as I got inside and turned around to watch the squirrels, I saw Tina.

*Uh, oh,* I thought, *did she see me out there? Will she tell Jimmy, and I'll get in trouble?*

She must not have. She didn't even look at me in the window. Instead, I think she only saw the open hole. "Oh, dear," she said. "I didn't know there was a hole here. And so deep! I'd better fill it in so no children will fall into it."

With her gardening shovel, Tina began to fill in the hole. But after a while, her movements slowed, and she seemed to be tired. I heard her say, "This is too much for me. I'll ask Jimmy or Joe if they can finish the job the next time I see one of them."

I'm glad she thought of that, because I sure didn't. If there's a next timeand I hope there isn't-I'll remember to do that. Safety is the first thing we have to think about.

I began to think about what just happened, and I felt good knowing that Candy promised not to scare us anymore, or hurt us. At least, I hope. Even more, I think Candy is becoming our friend. And that's an even better feeling.

## CHAPTER 11

# Jimmy Falls In Love

A few days went by, and I didn't see Candy or any other foxes around. Oddly, Squeaky and her crew weren't around too much, either. Jimmy had been working a lot of overtime. We still went outside, but not for long at all. Sometimes, Jimmy went right to sleep after dinner and our walk. He got up even earlier than before, and left in a hurry. All I heard was, "Rocket, see you later, have to run, love you." Just like that. I guessed he had a lot of work to do. At times, I overheard Jimmy talking to his friends on the phone, saying, "You have to take it while it's here."

But sometimes, when Jimmy came home late, there was that smell that's familiar to me. I just couldn't remember where I'd smelled it before.

The third night, he came home and said, like usual, "Hello, Rocket. I'm kind of tired today. Want to go bye-bye?"

Naturally, I did. So Jimmy put my leash on and we went for a walk.

As we were walking, I saw Tina walking toward us.

"Hi, Jimmy," she said. "How's Rocket?" She looked at me. "Oh, she's not barking."

"I think she's tired, Tina," Jimmy said, smiling. "Well, at least I know *I'm* tired."

"That's all right, Jimmy. I wanted to ask you if you knew anything about the hole in the back by the trees." *Uh, oh!*

Jimmy looked confused. "What hole, Tina?" "You don't know?" Jimmy shook his head.

"Come on Jimmy, I'll show you. I noticed it a few days ago."

Standing at the edge of the partially covered hole, Jimmy said, "Wow, who did this?"

"I don't know, Jimmy. I tried to cover it up myself, but there was so much dirt-"

"Oh, I'll take care of it," Jimmy said. "Where's the shovel?"

"I have one in the shed Jimmy. But you can wait till tomorrow."

"I don't know, Tina. That looks kind of deep. Someone might step into it and hurt their leg. I think it's better to finish it up now."

"Oh, Jimmy, you're not too tired, are you?"

"Well, I'm definitely tired. But I won't have time tomorrow."

"Okay. I'll go get the shovel, and be right back."

As Tina walked away, Jimmy turned to me and said, "Rocket, did you see anyone digging a hole while I was at work?" "Ruff!" *Oh, no, Jimmy, not me, no way!* "Humm. Okay. It was probably some kids." *Whew. Thanks, Tina.*

Tina returned with the shovel, and Jimmy filled in the hole.

"Jimmy, thank you so much. I didn't know what I was going to do."

"No problem, Tina. Anytime you need a hand, just let me know."

As Jimmy and I started walking back home, I was hoping he wasn't going to say anything about the hole. But when he opened the door, he looked at me, and said, "Hey, Rocket, are you up to something?" I just looked at him, looking sad.

He smiled at me. "No, that's silly. How could you have done something like that? You're a good girl. And, hey . . . if you *had* anything to do with it, I'm sure there was a good reason."

Jimmy fixed our dinner, but he still looked so tired. I hoped his overtime would end soon.

After dinner, Jimmy took his shirt off and threw it in the hamper. That smell came over me again. *He gets that smell at work, too?* I thought.

I guess he saw the funny look I gave him. "Hey, Rocket," he said, "I went over to my girlfriend's house before I came home. Just to help her out with a few things around the house. You know, she has a Golden Lab. Beautiful dog. She plays basketball with my girlfriend's sons. You'll meet her someday, okay?"

"Ruff! Ruff! Ruff! Ruff!"

After Jimmy left for work the next morning, I headed for the window. I hadn't seen any of the squirrels lately, but I really wanted to tell them about Tina finding the hole.

And this morning, they were there, right next to where the hole used to be, playing. They looked happy. No fear of Candy anymore.

I barked hello to them, and Squeaky came up to the window.

"Where you guys been?" I said.

"Oh, a lot's been happening, Rocket. We found a place. Not too far from here. There are nuts all over the place there."

"Well, I'm glad you came back, Squeaky. I thought you moved!"

Squeaky shook her head. "No, Rocket. This is our home, and we thank you for making it safe for us. We just like nuts, and sometimes we have to travel a long way to get ‚em."

"Well, you go back to what you were doing. I just wanted to make sure you guys hadn't moved or anything. Have you seen Candy anymore?"

"Yes, a couple of times. But every time, she just smiles and waves at us. We've even seen a few of her family members, and they're friendly, too. Cool, huh?"

"That's all we wanted," I said, relieved. "Maybe she'll turn out to be a good friend, after all."

Squeaky chuckled. "And in the woods, you can't have too many friends, can you?"

As Jimmy took off his shirt that night, that familiar smell came over me again. This time, when he threw it in the hamper, I went over to it and sniffed it for a long time. Still, I couldn't remember where I'd smelled it before. I knew that smell . . . I just knew it! But from when and where, I couldn't remember. It couldn't have been at the House of Misery, because I was the only dog there. And the Humane Society? No, I didn't think so. But at least once a week, I smelled that smell, and I wondered.

Summer moved on, and I guess I grew to be a full-sized dog. Oh, I still jumped and moved fast, but more and more often, I started to think before I jumped.

I didn't see too much of anyone around. Of course, I saw Jimmy every day, and sometimes Tina. But Jimmy was working a lot, sometimes not even coming home. I started going to the bathroom on the newspaper, but he told me it was all right. He talked a lot about his girlfriend, whose name was Eileen. Maybe he was staying there on the nights he didn't come home. I missed him, but I was glad he seemed happy. I loved Jimmy, and I knew he loved me.

I saw Candy around. Once, I saw an older fox that might have been Candy's father. She kept her promise, but I wondered sometimes if she got lonely. She was always alone, and no one ever played with her. Sometimes I'd go to the window and bark, and she howled back.

I can't remember exactly when, but I stopped seeing Squeaky or her crew for the longest time. Maybe they moved, and didn't tell me? Well, there weren't that many nuts around here anymore. Maybe they had to move a long way to find more. They didn't have an owner like Jimmy, so I guess they had to do what they had to do to survive.

But one day, there was a knock at the window. I ran into Jimmy's room, and saw MickeyNuts and Squeaky at the window!

"Hi, guys," I said.

"Hi, Rocket. We've been missing you."

"You missed me? It's me that missed you guys! Where you guys been? It looks like you guys are ten pounds heavier."

"We've been in Nutland," MickeyNuts said. "It's a long way from here. In Somers." "Somers? Where's that?"

Squeaky pointed. "It's that way."

"So is that where you guys have been all this time?"

MickeyNuts nodded. "And oh, we brought you something from there. The other guys are bringing it up."

"Hey, thanks. And oh, I've seen Candy around. She doesn't look too happy."

"Yeah, I know."

"What do you mean, *you know*, Mickey?"

"When we were going to Nutland, we passed Candy's family. They all seemed like they were having a good time." "What's wrong with that, Mickey?"

"Everyone but Candy. She was just standing there. Like she didn't want to play."

"It was more than that," Squeaky said. "Go ahead and tell Rocket."

MickeyNuts said, kind of slow, "They were making fun of her. Calling her a scaredy-cat for letting you and us bully her into leaving us alone."

"Oh, man," I said. "I didn't know. The couple of times I've seen her, she's acted friendly." I thought a minute, then said, "Look, maybe since were all here . . . the next time we see her, we'll play with her, okay? I mean . . . I wanted her to leave us alone, but I didn't think she would get in trouble with her family. The least we can do is try to be her friend."

MickeyNuts shrugged. "Okay, Rocket. Why not? Now that I'm not afraid that she'll eat me, I don't mind."

Some of the other squirrels came up, and their arms were full of nuts. They dropped them onto the porch roof.

"Hey, this is what we brought for you," Squeaky said.

"Wow, that's a lot of nuts! I'm happy you guys found a place like Somers. But . . . I wish it wasn't so far away."

I guess I must have looked as sad as I felt, because Squeaky said, "Hey, we'll still be able to come back and visit."

I nodded. "I guess so." Then I looked up at the sky. "Hey, guys, it's getting dark. Jimmy'll be home soon."

"Yeah, I guess we need to get out of here," Squeaky said. "But let me just say that you mean a lot to us, Rocket. And we'll never desert you. Never!"

"I love you guys, too. But now you gotta go. Jimmy'll go crazy if he sees you."

They all skittered off the porch, and I headed back inside.

Just as I heard Jimmy's car approaching, I looked out the window and saw Candy and MickeyNuts playing with each other, running around after each other. They saw me, and waved and smiled. I barked back. And I sure was relieved. Sure, I didn't want to be hurt or scared. But I didn't want Candy to suffer, just leave us alone. But as long as the squirrels were around, Candy would be all right.

Finally, I met Jimmy's girlfriend, Eileen. She had two boys, Timmy and Kenny, and a dog by the name of Daphne. I got to meet Eileen and the boys, but not Daphne yet. But I'm sure she'll be just as nice.

That all was good. But something else happened that wasn't so good. Jimmy started talking about moving back down to the Bronx, to be close to Eileen. I was sure I'd heard of that place before, but couldn't remember where. But I didn't think about it. Really, I couldn't think about it. I felt bad about the idea of moving. I'd met some good friends here. Yet sometimes, I guess you have to move on. And as long as I'm with Jimmy, I guess things will be good. I remembered when I met so many friends in the Humane Society. I didn't want to leave there, either. Even so, I adapted. And as long as I was with Jimmy, I would always have a better life than I did in the House of Misery.

One day, Jimmy came home from work and said, "Well, Rocket, it's time for us to talk to Tina. We're moving to the Bronx." *Bronx*. That name again. But there was no time to remember where I'd heard it before. Jimmy grabbed my leash, put it on me, and away we went to Tina's house.

"Oh, you're moving, Jimmy?" she said.

Jimmy nodded. "Yes, Tina. We really love it here, but we're moving down to the Bronx."

"So you can be closer to your work?"

"Yes. That," he smiled, "and a few other things. I've met someone."

Tina smiled back at him. "Oh, Jimmy, that's nice. I'll really miss you and Rocket, but I understand."

That night, Jimmy called me up onto the bed. I hopped up right next to him and lay on my back, and he started to rub my stomach. I love it when he does that.

"Rock, it looks like you've got lots of changes coming up," he said. "Next month, we'll be moving to the Bronx. I have an appointment with a guy to see an apartment. I'm sorry I'm moving you around a lot. Hopefully, things will work out with Eileen, and we can maybe live together as one family someday. I love being with her, and being with you. I'll be closer to JJ, too." He smiled. "I have to stop calling him that. He's pretty big now. But no matter what, wherever I go, you'll go."

Long after he put me down and went to bed, I carried a feeling of pure happiness and love. I started to think about all the good things that had happened to me. Meeting King and his gang, all the friends I made at the Humane Society. Meeting Squeaky, MickeyNuts, and all the squirrels. Even Candy turned out to be a friend!

But still, no one likes to leave their friends, and I didn't either.

Soon, I felt tears sliding down my snout. I tried to distract myself by wondering where I'd heard of "the Bronx" before, but it was no good. The tears just kept falling.

I heard a knock at the window. Squeaky was there, tapping softly with her paw.

"Rocket, why are you crying?" Squeaky said. "What's the matter?"

"Well, Squeaky . . . Jimmy, my owner, decided to move to the Bronx."

"The Bronx? Why?"

"So he could be closer to his girlfriend and to work."

"Hey, I'm sorry to hear that. But . . . as long as he's happy, maybe it'll be good for you, right?"

"Yeah, I guess so. But I'm going to miss you guys."

"We'll miss you, too, Rocket. After all you did for us, we'll miss you a lot."

"Squeaky?" "Yeah?"

"I . . . it'll be hard to tell the others. Could you-?" "Oh, sure, I'll tell them for you. No problem."

"Thanks. And . . . I'll try to look at this as a good thing. I hope it is. I . . . I don't even think they have trees in the Bronx."

"Oh, no, Rocket. They do have trees. And big fields, too. The Bronx is very nice. They have parks, and exciting things to do."

I looked at her, confused. "How do you know so much about the Bronx?"

"My cousins live there, in Van Cortland Park. They come up once in a while and tell me what's going on."

Hearing what Squeaky said, I felt a little better. Not much, but a little.

As we walked around Deerhaunt Drive, I could see Squeaky and her crew hopping from one tree to the next. We saw Tina. And the trees. *Oh, I hope Squeaky is right about a lot of trees in the Bronx!* I thought.

As we went back to the apartment, Jimmy saw Joe, who lived on the first floor.

"Hey, Joe, how you been?" Jimmy called out. "Good, Jimmy, what's up?"

I'll be moving by the end of the month. You want to make a few dollars? I'll need help to move. I've got a couple of friends who'll help, but they might have to work."

"Sure," Joe said. "But you don't have to pay me. You've been a good neighbor, and I hate to see you go."

"Thanks," Jimmy said. "But I insist on giving you something. I've got some stuff I might have to leave. You can take a look at it, and keep what you want of it."

"Sounds good to me," Joe said. "Just let me know when."

Jimmy liked the apartment, and all was arranged for us to move at the end of the month. When moving day came, Joe knocked on our door. "Hey, Jimmy," he said. "I have the truck. Let's get things going."

Jimmy and Joe moved boxes and furniture into the truck, laughing and talking. I mostly watched and barked. After a while, I got bored and went to Jimmy's window. I could see Squeaky, MickeyNuts, and all the other squirrels out there, looking sad. Even Candy was out there, and they were all looking at me.

I glanced at the door. Joe or Jimmy had left it opened, so I slipped out of it and walked down the stairs. I could hear Joe telling Jimmy, "Your dog is walking out of the house."

Jimmy looked at me, then at the trees. "That's all right. She's just going to say good-bye to her friends."

"What, her friends?" Joe said. "Wow, Jimmy, I never saw so many squirrels around here. Hey, look at that fox. Rocket might get hurt."

I looked at Jimmy, just sure he would call me back. Instead, he smiled at me and said, "Don't worry, Joe. I don't know how I know, but I think that's Rocket's friend."

Joe scratched his chin. "Even the fox?"

"Yeah. Rocket knows all of them. And I think that's why she's a little sad."

As I approached Squeaky and the others I said, "Hey guys, I'll miss all of you and I'll never forget you."

In their own way, all thirty or forty of them said the same back to me.

"Squeaky, I'll especially miss you. It was you who gave me courage when I was abandoned by my first family, so long ago." "Hey, it's okay," Squeaky said. "In the same situation, you would have done the same thing for me."

"You know," I said. "I guess what's bothering me most is that I've never heard anything about King. I mean, all I know is that, when I was at the Humane Society, this man from Hunts Point adopted him."

"Hey, guess what?" Squeaky said.

I turned to her.

"Hunts Point is in the Bronx."

*That* was where I'd heard that name before!

"Gee, wouldn't that be nice, meeting up with him again?" I said. "But . . . even if I did, he probably won't even remember me." "I doubt that," Squeaky said. "Once anybody meets you, they never forget you."

I sighed. "That's nice of you to say that, Squeaky, but who knows?"

"And hey, moving down to the Bronx might be good for you,"

Squeaky said, trying to cheer me up. "You just have to watch all the cars and trucks. There a lot of people there, too." She patted my head and gave me an encouraging smile. "Knowing you, Rocket, all the dogs, cats, and squirrels there will all want to know you. You'll see."

I heard someone calling, and it was Candy. I went over to her, and we hugged.

And then I heard Jimmy calling me.

# CHAPTER 12

# Rocket & The Bronx

Jimmy and Joe were still putting the last boxes on the truck, so I climbed back up the stairs. The apartment was so empty. I walked to where my bed had been and looked at it. I glanced at the window, but didn't have the heart to look out of it. That was for the best, I thought.

Jimmy and Joe emerged from the kitchen, and Jimmy said, "Okay, Rock, everything's ready. Tina's coming over to say goodbye, so come on."

Tina was standing beside the truck, and said goodbye. She gave me several pats, and I could see tears behind her glasses. I'll miss her, almost as much as I miss the apartment. It was hard not to cry, but I managed not to.

As we were driving, I heard Joe ask Jimmy, "So, how is the Bronx? How's the area we're going to?"

"The Bronx is nice, I guess," Jimmy replied. "Wherever you make your bed, it's as good as you make it." Hey, I *really* agreed with that!

"The area I'm moving to is where I use to live before moving up to Croton," Jimmy continued. "Morris Park. It's a nice area. A lot of attached homes. Not like Croton. It has a lot more people."

"Yeah, I've heard of that area," Joe said. "Aren't there some junkyards down there? I'm always looking for spare parts for this old truck."

"Yeah, there are," Jimmy replied. "Hunts Point has a lot of them. If one doesn't have what you want, go up or down the block and go to another one, and you get what you need." He chuckled. "Kind of like a shopping mall for spare parts. So, what do you need?"

"I need a mirror for the driver's side," Joe said.

Jimmy looked. "Yeah, I noticed you didn't have one. They'll give you a ticket for that, you know."

"Yeah, that's why I was hoping I could find one today."

"After we drop the furniture off, let's head over there," Jimmy said.

"Sounds good to me."

The unloading went faster than the loading. I didn't see the apartment then. I just stayed in the truck. And then, we headed for the junkyards.

The first place we stopped was Mike's Junkyard. Jimmy said, "Joe, just go inside, and ask for Mike."

"What? You're not going to come with me?" Joe nodded out his window.

"Why? They're not going to bite you."

I followed Joe's gaze and saw five big dogs playing around on the sidewalk.

"Okay, okay," Jimmy said. "I'll come in with you. Rocket, you stay right here."

Like, do I have anywhere else to go?

I saw Jimmy and Joe walk inside the office. About two seconds later, I heard a knock on the window. I turned around and saw a huge Great Dane. His head was as big as my whole body. I went over to the window, and up came a German Shepherd.

I put my paw on the window. The Great Dane and the Shepherd did the same, and we just looked at each other. I put my nose to the window as if to say hello. They did the same. I felt good. I'd never seen a Great Dane before, but the German Shepherd reminded me of King. And that's what really felt good.

"Down, girl, down!"

I looked over to see Jimmy and Joe coming toward the truck.

They climbed in, and Joe said, "Hey, Jimmy, the dogs were all overthe truck."

"Sure, they were saying hello to Rocket."

Joe chuckled, then said, "So, where is Gepeto's?" "Just around the corner." My mind started flying. *Gepeto. Hunts Point. The Bronx.*

"That's it!" I barked. "King and Prince were adopted by a Mr. Gepeto!" "Hey, settle down, girl," Jimmy said, and put his hand on my head.

I stopped barking, but my mind never stopped thinking. *Oh, my, I might see King and Prince! I don't believe this!*

Joe started up the truck, and drove around the corner. A big sign read "Gepeto's Junkyard of Hunts Point." Joe pulled up, Joe and Jimmy opened the doors, and I snuck out.

"Where you going, Rock?" Jimmy said.

I whimpered. He just *had* to let me come with him!

Finally, Jimmy smiled at me and said, "Okay, but stay close."

As Jimmy and Joe went into the office, I started looking all around for King and Prince. Jimmy and Joe went to the office and rang a bell. Out Mr.

Gepeto walked . . . and oh, my gracious, it's not just King, it's Prince too!

They started barking and running toward me, and me to them.

"Smallone, Smallone!" they called out. I was too excited to correct them. We started hopping around and playing, running after each other, barking, and just so happy to see each other again.

I could hear Jimmy saying to Joe, "Look at that, Joe."

"Wow, Jimmy," Joe replied, "look at Rocket. All the big dogs love her."

Jimmy looked at the dogs and a big grin crossed his face. "Sure they do. She knows them. And so do I!"

Jimmy started to explain, but Mr. Gepeto walked up then. "I'm Mr. Gepeto. May I help you?"

"Yes, please," Jimmy said. "We're looking for a side mirror for my friend's pickup truck. Just like that one over there."

"Take what you need. I'll be in the office." "Thank you, Mr. Gepeto."

I saw Joe walk up to them. "Excuse me. I have a mirror and an oil cap. How much?"

Mr. Gepeto told him, "That'll be twenty dollars," and Joe handed him some money.

"Excuse me, Mr. Gepeto," Jimmy said, with a weird smile on his face. "Where did you get your dogs?"

"I adopted them from the Humane Society of Connecticut." Mr. Gepeto looked at me. "Say, your Chihuahua looks familiar. Where did you get her?"

"The same place you got yours-The Humane Society of Connecticut."

"Boy, isn't that a coincidence," Mr. Gepeto said. "That's why they're all happy and playing. They all know each other from there."

Then he turned his attention back to Jimmy. "So, what brings you to the Bronx?"

"I'm moving to Morris Park."

"That's nice. Maybe you can bring your dog over sometimes." "I'd like that," Jimmy said.

Hey, I would too! "Ruff! Ruff! Ruff!"

They kept talking, and so did I. Oh, boy, did I!

"Hey, Rocket," King said. "Have you heard anything about Blackie and Lady?"

"Oh, they're doing fine," I said. "As a matter of fact, everyone that was in the show that day is doing great. Even the cats!" "How are Minsk and Beauty?"

"Good. Minsk lived down the road from us at our old place. But we had to move from there. I've talked to her, and she's doing good. So is Beauty.

Minsk's owner's sister has her and loves her."

"Happy to hear that," Prince said.

I heard Jimmy say, "Okay, Mr. Gepeto. We have to run. Moving day and all. I'll be seeing you."

Mr. Gepeto smiled. "Okay, guys. Come back and say hello anytime."

Oh, man, I didn't want to go. Not so soon! I turned to King and Prince and said, "Hey guys have to run. It was nice seeing you again, and I'm glad you're all right."

"Bye, Smallone," King said.

"Oh, yeah, I forgot to tell you. Call me Rocket. That's what my owner named me, and I like it better."

King nodded. "Nice name. But you'll always be Smallone to us."

Smiling, Prince said, "Yeah! Smallone, we've missed you."
"Me, too," I said.

"Aw, look at that," I heard Joe say. "It's like they're saying goodbye to Rocket." He sighed and added, "Sometimes I wish I had a pet."

"Well, you already know that Tina won't mind," Jimmy said, and chuckled. "Unlike the landlady I had when I first got Rocket. If you want one, you should go to the Humane Society of Connecticut. See Gail or Terry. Tell her you know Smallone-that's Rocket's old name-and they'll get you a great pet."

He turned to me and said, "Come on, Rock, up, up."

We all climbed into the truck, Joe started it up, and then started steering it along the busy street.

"Hey, Rocket, seen some of your friends uh?" Jimmy said. "They came from the same place where I adopted you." "Ruff! Ruff! Ruff!" *I know, I know!*

The apartment, which Jimmy had rented from someone named Tony, was a little bigger than where we used to live. And it had a window to look out of. That part was okay.

Back at the apartment, I watched Jimmy and Joe bring all the stuff in.

"Is that it?" I heard Joe ask.

"That's it, Joe. Not too bad. It's only 6:30."

"Yeah, good time," Joe agreed. "I guess I'd better be heading back. Jimmy, anytime you need a hand in anything, just let me know."

Before Joe left, he looked at me for a long time, then said, "Jimmy, there's something about that dog. She's like a little human."

Jimmy nodded. "Yeah, I know. That's why I love her so much. I feel like I have a little daughter on my hands."

When Joe left, Jimmy turned around several times and said, "Wow, Rocket, here we are. In the Bronx." He looked at me and smiled. "Pretty noisy, huh?"

"Ruff! Ruff!"

"Let me put some things together, then I'll take you out for your first walk in the Bronx. There's a lot of dogs around here. I think Eileen might bring Daphne over later. I think you'll like her. She's a Golden Lab."

And then, I had my first walk in the Bronx. I don't know what came over me. I didn't feel too good. Too many people; the cars, buses, and trucks; not much grass. All I could do was flop down on the sidewalk. I didn't think I was going like it here. What was I going to do?

Well, like I always do. I'll give it some time. I'll make it work for Jimmy and me. Jimmy's happy, and when he's happy, I should be happy. So I'll give it a try.

I picked myself up and started walking. Jimmy saw some friends, and they talked a bit. We said our goodbyes and walked back to the apartment. When we got inside, the phone was ringing. Jimmy talked a moment, then turned to me. "Hey, Rock, how's dinner sound at Eileen's house?

JJ's already over there-he goes there after school most days. And you're invited."

"Ruff! Ruff!"

Laughing, he told Eileen, "Sounds like a plan. . . . Seven o'clock? That'll be fine. See you then." Then he turned to me and said, "Hey, Rock, you're going to meet Daphne."

Jimmy set up my bed, and I laid down in it. And finally, a nice feeling came over me. Now that we were close to Eileen, maybe Jimmy would be home more often.

Before I knew it, he was parking the car, and we were walking up the driveway toward a house. Eileen was walking toward us, and a Golden Lab ran beside her. And finally, I recognized that smell. That little dog that used to rest her head on mine was now almost as big as King! When I was at the Humane Society, I heard about a lady with two boys who was interested in Goldie, the Golden Lab puppy. Now I knew that the lady's name was Eileen, and Daphne was the Golden Lab!

I always wondered what happened to her, and now, I knew! She was so small back then, but now, she was three times bigger than me. But of course she'd have to be bigger than she was. It had been, what? Over a year.

"Jimmy, Rocket," Eileen said over my barking. "Come on in. The boys are playing in the back. And Jimmy, come inside. I need you to help me with something. I've been waiting for you."

A boy came running around the side of the house, yelling, "Come on, Daphne!"

Eileen laughed. "That's Kenny." Kenny was a slim kid with black hair and brown eyes. His hair was slicked back. JJ ran up with him.

Jimmy and Eileen went inside, and there we stood: me, and the Golden Lab that laid in my lap when Dr. Casey brought her to my cage. Wow.

"Let's play ball!" Kenny yelled. "Hey, Rocket, you too."

Daphne and I followed Kenny. They were all playing basketball, and I was so surprised when Daphne passed the ball to JJ with her nose!

Another boy came up to me. "Hi, Rocket, my name's Tim." Tim was a little heavier than Kenny, but shared the same dark eyes and black hair. His hair was slicked back, too.

Just as he said his name, I saw the ball coming my way, heading straight for JJ. Moving fast, I ran toward the ball and kicked it.

"Yeah, Rocket, that's the way," JJ said. Then, to the other two boys, he said, "I told you she was a fast learner. And strong, too!"

We all had a great time, if in a different way than I ever had before. And suddenly, I was beginning to like this place called the Bronx.

We played for a while, and Daphne and I got very tired. So I was glad when I heard Eileen call out, "Come on boys, time to eat. And hey, go get washed up. What happened to your clothes and hands?"

"It was Kenny and Rocket against me and Daphne, and JJ was the referee," Tim said. "So who won?"

Tim pointed to Kenny, then me. "They did." "Rocket and Kenny beat you?

But Rocket's so lit-" "Yeah, I know. Right."

Eileen turned to Jimmy. "Rocket plays basketball?" Jimmy laughed. "I guess she does now."

You bet! "Ruff! Ruff! Ruff!"

When Kenny and Timmy went inside, I ask Daphne if she remembered King and Prince.

She shook her head. "I guess it was because I was so young. I just remember Dr. Casey. How long have you been with Jimmy, Rocket?"

"About a year or so. So, Daphne, did you ever live in the country with a lot of trees, grass, dirt roads and stuff? And could just walk around anytime you felt like it?"

She shook her head. "I've been here ever since I can remember."

"Don't get me wrong, Daphne. It's nice here. You have parks, trees, and a lot more friends to choose from. But the country is nice. You have to go there sometime."

Eileen came out and brought us some food and water. It was good. It was table food-chicken and rice, which I love. Daphne and I ate, and we talked a bit. The apartment where she lives was kind of small, but she says it's all right for them.

Most important, I found my little friend. And I'll be able to see her anytime Jimmy is at Eileen's. I'll be able to see King and Prince whenever Jimmy needs spare parts, too.

After dinner, Daphne and I watched Jimmy and Eileen laughing and talking with Tim, JJ and Kenny. Daphne was curled up, just like I remembered her. In that, she was still a puppy. A big puppy, but still a puppy.

*This is how things are supposed to be*, I thought. *Having fun, enjoying your life, and making each day count.*

Daphne and I went into the boys' room, where they were getting ready for bed. Tim and Kenny climbed into their bed, and Kenny called out, "Daphne, you know the deal."

Daphne looked down at me, kissed me on the nose. "It was great seeing you again." And then she hopped up on Kenny's bed.

I looked at them, she looked at me, and she said, "Rocket, I will always love you for the way you looked after me at the Humane Society. Dr. Casey told me all about it. Said you had a lot to do with the television show being such a success."

I was glad to hear Jimmy calling me. I didn't think I could hear anymore without crying. And I sure didn't want to do that in front of Daphne.

I ran to Jimmy and Eileen. Eileen picked me up, kissed me on the head and said, "Don't be a stranger, Rocket."

"Eileen, thanks for dinner and everything," Jimmy said. "I had a great time.

And thanks for letting JJ spend the night. I'll call you later." "Drive safe," she said, and I swear I saw a tear in her eye.

Jimmy opened the car door, then walked around to get in the driver's seat.

As he was settling in, he said, "Rocket, did you have a good time?"

My tail was wiggling and I went "Ruff! Ruff! Ruff!"

He smiled at me. "You know, for a while, I was worried that you didn't like it here. But you look happy now."

As he drove home, he told me that he and Eileen were thinking about getting married. "Not now," he said, "but in time."

I started to think that if they got married, we'd all live together. And I wasn't so sure I liked that. I have Jimmy, and he has me, and we're happy together. Daphne is nice and everything, Eileen and the boys are great, but I don't want to live with anybody else. I have my home, and that's with Jimmy. I don't think Daphne would like that, either. I mean, playing ball and visiting sometimes is one thing. But she probably feels the same way I do.

*Well, we'll see what happens*, I finally decided. *If there's love, there's nothing I can't do.*

I thought Jimmy would be home more often since we lived close by. I didn't think I would see him less. But the longer we lived in the Bronx, the less I saw him. He'd come home, take me out for a minute or two, just so I could do my business. And that was it. He was always either working late, or over at Eileen's house.

He kept telling me that if we had a house with more room, maybe we could all live together. Then he'd say, "But Eileen would like to wait till we're married."

To be honest, I didn't know what to say when he said that except "Ruff!"

More time went by, and things didn't get better. And now, I wondered if Daphne was getting jealous because I was at her house a lot. I mean, it was her home. I wouldn't like it if another dog came around and was around Jimmy all the time. And, I'll admit, I was a little jealous when I saw Jimmy playing with Daphne. I pretended it didn't bother me, but it did. And there was a lot of noise at Daphne's house, too. with hardly any room to get away from it for a while.

One night, Timmy went to pet me on the head, and Daphne showed her teeth at me. He said, "No, Daphne! Don't show your teeth at Rocket. Be a good girl."

But I felt scared, like I used to feel in the House of Misery. I didn't ever want to feel that way again, and now I did, if just for that second.

*Daphne's a great dog, and she's only protecting her home,* I'd tell myself. *And maybe, in time, things will change.*

Or maybe, *I* could change. Maybe, if I didn't go over there, Daphne would be happier. I was happy for her that she had a home, and that she felt wanted. It's good to feel wanted. So maybe if I didn't come around as much, things would be better for Daphne, and for Jimmy.

But the more time passed, it seemed the worse things got between me and Daphne. She started teasing me a lot, and sniffing at me when I didn't want her to. Tonight, she did it again, and I showed my teeth back at her and growled. I mean, she was five times my size, and I had to do something!

Eileen and Jimmy noticed, and broke us up. When Jimmy got to me, I put my two front paws up and he picked me up. He seemed mad, and I felt terrible about that. I don't think he liked Daphne at that moment.

He put my leash on, said goodbye to Eileen, and we left. It was the first time that Eileen didn't say, "I love you" before he left.

In the car, Jimmy told me he was sorry Daphne showed her teeth and barked at me. He thought it was because I snapped at her, and he didn't blame me for snapping. "Hey, if a Lab was sniffing my butt, I'd snap at them too," he said. He laughed, and I did too, and licked his face and hands. "Easy Rock, easy," he said.

Neither of us said anything for a while, but then he said,

"Rocket, you have bad days and good days. This was a bad day,

„cause your feelings were hurt. You can take the bad day and sob, or you can take the bad day and make it a good day. It's up to you."

And then the weirdest thing happened. He grinned at me and said, "With Daphne, here's how you do that-every time you see Daphne, make sure you're sitting down. Hey, you're so big and mean-looking, maybe she's scared of you."

And he started laughing, like it was some kind of big joke!

I'll admit it. I got mad at him. I wished I could talk! Then I'd tell him that even if *he* thinks it's funny, it wasn't very funny to *me*. I look at him laughing and driving, and people in other cars were just looking at him. So I barked: "Ruff! Ruff! Ruff!"

"I know, Rocket, I know," he blurted out, "but that's so funny." I wanted to tell him, "Did you notice *I'm* not laughing?"

He grabbed me up and kissed me on the head. Now, I'm feeling like maybe it *was* funny, after all. Oh, man, what am I going to do?

## CHAPTER 13

# Jimmy & Rocket, Eileen & Daphne

As soon as we walked into the apartment, the phone rang. "Hello? Hi, Eileen. . . . No, don't be sorry. Rocket had a great time with Daphne. You want to hear her?" He turned to me and held out the phone.

"Rocket, speak."

"Ruff! Ruff! Ruff!"

He put the phone back to his ear. "You see? She had a great time. And so did I. . . . No, no problem. I'll call you tomorrow." I saw him smile, then he said, "Bye. Love you," right before hanging up the phone.

Later, I lay in my bed, watching Jimmy getting ready for bed. I couldn't help but wonder what would happen if Jimmy and Eileen got married. *If he marries her,* I thought, *then we have to live together. And Daphne doesn't really like me.*

Even worse, I felt like I was losing Jimmy. I wished it were the way it was before. Just him and me. I began to feel like I was all alone, even when at Daphne's crowded house. I guess Daphne got tired of being spoken to every time she bothered me. After a while, she started acting like she didn't even know me. And sometimes, even though I said I wouldn't, I found myself snapping at her to let me be by myself. But I knew Jimmy loved her and the boys.

But most of the time, things were good with Daphne. I had to remember that. I also had to remember that she was still a puppy. Just a kid, like I used to be. I decided to give it some time.

I don't know when the change began, but one morning, when I opened my eyes, a feeling came over me. I started to feel good that Jimmy was happy. It was more than that. It was that I finally accepted I would have to share him.

Even more, that sharing him would be all right, as long as he loved me and wanted me with him. No matter how many dogs or people came into our lives, I was certain that love wouldn't change.

I was just sure that I could have Jimmy, and let Jimmy have a life, too. I made up my mind to always try to be nice to Daphne. *Who knows?* I thought. *Maybe we'll become friends again.*

I looked up to see Jimmy getting ready for work. When he picked up the leash, I ran to him and put my two front paws up on his leg-to reach up to him, so he wouldn't have to bend down to put my leash.

"Hey, you're looking pretty cheerful this morning," he said. His faced held a kind of relieved look. The same way I felt when I left the House of Misery. And that made me certain that whatever I had to do to make him happy, it was worth it.

He left for work like usual, but this time, I heard his footsteps stop in the hallway. And I heard him saying, "I always take her out. She never does her business in the house. So it's not Rocket you smell. Bye, Tony, I'm running a little late I'll talk to you later."

Tony? That was Jimmy's landlord. I hope he wasn't mad at me. I didn't do anything in the hall. Always outside.

The bad feeling came back, and I went to the window. But this time, there was no Squeaky, Candy or anybody else. All I saw were windows to other houses.

*I have to stop this!* I thought. *I have to be grateful for what I have, and make the best of it.*

I heard Jimmy's key in the door.

Almost as soon as Jimmy came inside, the doorbell rang. It was Tony "Jimmy, I hate to do this, but I have to ask you to get rid of your dog."

"Rocket? But why? You said it was all right."

"I know, but the smell is getting too much, and my wife has decided she doesn't want any pets in the house."

"It's not Rocket. I take her out all the time. Not less then three times a day.

And now I've moved in, and you want me to get rid of my dog?"

"Come on," Tony said. "Jimmy, I'm sorry, but my wife-"

"Tony, I'm sorry, but I can't do that. If she leaves, I have to leave too. I'll be out by the end of the month." "Sorry, Jimmy." "Yeah, right," Jimmy muttered.

The door closed, and Jimmy turned to me, his face sad. "Rocket, we'll be moving again. But don't worry. We'll be fine. We just have to find a place." I went over to Jimmy, and he rubbed my head.

"Hey, Rocket, we've been through a lot of changes. Guess what? We have to go through a little more. Tough times don't last, but tough people and dogs do. I don't know where we'll be going, but we'll be together. If I can't find anything, I'll ask Eileen. Maybe we could stay there till we get something, okay?"

Well, if I had to choose between being homeless, and having Daphne as a roommate, I would choose Daphne. "Ruff! Ruff! Ruff!"

"Oh, you like that idea?" "Ruff!"

"Good. I'll talk to Eileen later. As soon as I get off work, I'll call her."

He came home from work in good time, took me for a quick walk, made some dinner, and put a movie on. Then he called Eileen. "... the end of the month," he was saying. "That's great ... I'll talk to you later."

# ROCKET & THE CONSTRUCTION WORKER

As soon as he hung up, he turned to me and said, "Hey, Rocket, we're going to move in with Eileen and the boys and Daphne. This time next month, we'll be there. It'll be kind of cramped till we get another place, but let's try it."

"Ruff! Ruff! Ruff!"

A few weeks later, Jimmy came home and said, "Rocket, I'm going to start bringing some things over to Eileen's. First the boxes, then the big stuff on Friday."

Friday came quick. All too soon, I was looking at yet-another empty apartment while Jimmy took the last load to Eileen's house. And even though Jimmy said he'd be right back, I wondered if he would. It was definitely a low point in this dog's life. But at least I wouldn't miss this apartment as much as I missed the one where Tina lived. And where Squeaky lived.

After a while, Jimmy stuck his head in the door. "Hey, there you are!" he said. "I thought I forgot something." *Ha, ha.*

Maybe living with Daphne and her family would turn out to be nice after all. I hoped so. At least Jimmy looked happy about it.

I'll admit it. By the time we got inside Eileen's house, I was so nervous, I did something I hadn't done since I was a puppy in the House of Misery.

"No," Eileen yelled. "Jimmy, she's going to the bathroom on the floor!"

"I'll clean it up," Jimmy said, his voice calm. "She's nervous, you know.

New environment. She'll be all right."

"I hope so, Jimmy," she said. "No, Daphne, leave her alone!"

A little while later, Eileen said, "Jimmy, your dog is all over you."

Funny, she used to call me by my name. Now I'm suddenly, "your dog."

"Chihuahuas are very attached to their owners," Jimmy said. "She'll be fine. Could you let her stay in our room?"

Eileen sighed. "All right. Make a bed for her over there, Jimmy. But don't you think Daphne might get jealous? 'Cause I don't even let Daphne stay in my room."

"Hope not, Eileen."

I wish I could say things got better, but they didn't. After a while, I wondered how much longer I could stay here like this. Jimmy got up and went to work. Daphne was always eating my food and drinking all the water that Eileen left out for us. Eileen went to work, and I stayed in the room. Oh, I could have gone outside of it, but I didn't want to deal with Daphne, 'cause I really don't think she wanted me there. And I knew Jimmy loved Eileen, but I don't think he was happy anymore.

Some time went by, and one day, Jimmy came home acting happy. He was laughing with Eileen and the boys. Even I was laughing and barking. It seemed like for once, we were all having fun.

Daphne got pretty excited, and started to bark at me. It wasn't a nice bark, either. I showed my teeth, but before I could run away, she picked me up in her mouth!

I could hear Jimmy and Eileen both saying, "Stop it! Daphne, stop!"

Things happened so fast after that. I don't know how or when, but suddenly, I wasn't in Daphne's mouth anymore.

"Eileen, get your dog out of here," Jimmy said. "Outside, Daphne! You're bad. NO! Don't do that to Rocket! Bad girl!"

At almost the same time, Eileen looked at me. I didn't move. I was too scared.

"Eileen," Jimmy said with a sigh. "My dog could get killed the next time that happens."

After a while, they sat down, and I heard them talking.

"It hasn't been nice here for either of us," Jimmy said. "The boys aren't happy. I'm not happy. You're not happy, and the dogs aren't happy. I still love you, Eileen, but maybe the timing isn't right." "I told you that, Jimmy," Eileen said.

Jimmy nodded. "Yes, you did. And you were right. I'll start looking for a place."

"Okay," Eileen said. "Jimmy, I still love you."

"And I love you, Eileen. I'll get a place close-by, and we can try to make everyone happy."

Eileen smiled at him. "That's the idea, Jimmy."

He put his arm around her. "Thank you for understanding."

"Of course I do! I wouldn't want Daphne living in fear or getting hurt." "Yeah, I know." But his eyes were still sad.

A few days after Daphne bit me, Jimmy came in and told me that he'd found another place, in Morris Park. "It's not as big as this one, but it'll do until we get a place big enough for all of us. And the best part is, we can move in right away."

And that sounded wonderful to me. "Ruff! Ruff! Ruff!"

Daphne and I were able to make up by moving day. Things were still a little tense, but I think she regretted what she did, and was sorry.

Our new place was in the basement of a big house. Eileen helped us move, and some of Jimmy's friends. That was nice.

After we settled in, Jimmy and I walked to the corner store. Guess what was the best thing? Every dog I saw was little, like me. In fact, some of them were even smaller than I was. I got close enough to one of them to smell him, and I even let him smell me.

Everything was good with Eileen again. Sometimes, she'd come and take me for walks. When she did, she would pick me up and kiss me on the head. So that's how I knew things were okay again.

A little time went by, and Jimmy and Eileen seemed to be getting along really well. Soon, he told me that he and Eileen had decided to buy a house-a big house, with room for all of us. And his sad face turned happy again.

Now, when Eileen came over, she brought Daphne with her. I was glad. I was beginning to miss Daphne. One day, I was lying next to Daphne while Jimmy and Eileen talked. As they talked, I kept hearing the word "Buchanan," but didn't pay much attention.

The next time I heard the word "Buchanan, it was one day when Jimmy came home and said, "Hey, Rocket, Eileen and I are going to take a look at this house tomorrow. It's in Buchanan. You know where that is? Near where we used to live. One town up. Close enough to say hello to Tina and Bobby and all your friends. Keep your paws crossed, okay?"

Would I? You bet! "Ruff! Ruff! Ruff!"

The next day, Jimmy came in all excited. "Hey, Rocket," he said, "I found a house. I put the security deposit down, and we're moving in June first." He stopped, then laughed. "I think I better tell Eileen about this . . . what do you say?"

"Ruff! Ruff!"

He went to the phone, and I saw the same joy in his eyes as the day he took me home from the Humane Society.

Jimmy left to meet up with Eileen-she wanted to see the house.

He didn't come back until very late. He still looked happy.

"Rocket," he said, "we're moving. It's a big house with four bedrooms, apple trees in the back, and a studio where we could put a pool table if we wanted."

I had no idea what a pool table and studio were, or the washer and dryer he talked about, but if it made him this happy, I was thrilled for him! I started barking.

He made arrangements with someone named Kevin, and that was it-on Friday, we're moving!

# CHAPTER 14

# Home

That was the craziest moving day I ever lived through. Eileen's kids helped, but between her place and Jimmy's, there was a lot of stuff to move. Every time I saw one of them, they had a box in their arms. After what seemed like hours, Jimmy picked me up, put me in the car, and away we went, a car-and truck caravan.

The house was beautiful, just like Jimmy described. A really big house, with three floors. And of course, I love it here.

Every now and then, Jimmy takes me for a ride to see Tina. After we visit with her, we walk around, and most times, I see Squeaky and her family. Candy comes around sometimes, too. I'd like to take Daphne there someday, but Jimmy and Eileen like to keep one of us at home when nobody's there.

Sometimes I rest my head on my paws and think of the days at the Humane Society. And I think about the time before that-a time I'd like to forget, but never will be able to. Or maybe I shouldn't forget about the House of Misery. After all, it brought me to where I am today, and was the beginning of what led me to King and to all my friends, and to Jimmy and Eileen.

Nowadays, I try to be a good watchdog, to love my family and friends, and to be kind to everyone I meet. I believe there is nothing wasted in life. I also believe there are people and dogs, cats and other animals that don't feel the same way that I do, and

I must remember that. And I can never forget that there are many cats and dogs that don't have a home, and will never have a home.

But me, I'm finally home.

## ABOUT THE AUTHOR

Jmmy Stalikas is a construction worker living in New York, and Rocket was his beloved pet, adopted from the Humane Society of Connecticut.

www.ingramcontent.com/pod-product-compliance
Ingram Content Group UK Ltd.
Pitfield, Milton Keynes, MK11 3LW, UK
UKHW022226230426